Burning Leaves

Bernard Marin

First published by Busybird Publishing 2024

ISBN:
Paperback: 978-1-923216-56-3
Ebook: 978-1-923216-57-0

Cover image: pexels-dharmpal-jharwal-meena-81016632-8779732

Cover design: Busybird Publishing

Layout and typesetting: Rebecca Cannizzaro/ Busybird Publishing

Busybird Publishing
2/118 Para Road
Montmorency, Victoria
Australia 3094
www.busybird.com.au

For my wife, Wendy,
daughters Amy and Rachel,
daughter-in-law Deb, son-in-law Joel,
and grandchildren Goldie, Ziggy, Millie and Andie.

Author's Note

While I have endeavoured to be rigorous in my research, I make no claim as to the factual accuracy of my portrayal of the historical figures mentioned in each story.

The encounters and conversations that appear in this book are works of the author's imagination, and the characters are not intended to bear any resemblance to any person now living.

Like all historical fiction, the narratives in this book draw inspiration from the lives of the main characters while retaining sufficient artistic licence to enliven the stories as the author interprets and sees fit.

Contents

Dealing with the Devil

'I've been reading a really interesting book,' Solly said as he took a sip of his coffee.

'Tell me more,' said David.

They were sitting in their favourite haunt, a Brighton café where their usual fare was either blueberry muffins or strawberry crepes washed down with cappuccinos. Opposite was a row of California bungalows, with large front lawns and neatly pruned azaleas, camellias and hydrangeas.

Outside it was raining and a cold autumn wind whistled through the half-open café door. Leaves tumbled from the plane trees, to be picked up and danced in circles by the wind then dumped in the gutter.

Solly and David, both retired solicitors, had been partners in private practice since graduating from Melbourne Law School in the late fifties. Together they had built a large, well-respected legal firm specialising in tax and commercial law. Their expertise was sought by wealthy Jewish individuals, families, and large companies, both private and publicly listed.

They were men in their sixties. Solly was tall and well built, clad in a white silk shirt, beige cashmere jumper, tan trousers, and a new pair of tennis sneakers. He had a square jaw and a narrow face, his thinning brown hair covered in part by a knitted yarmulka. He stared at David, his blue eyes sharp behind black-framed glasses.

David looked older than Solly. He had sparse grey hair and his dark eyes were set in deep sockets. His cheekbones were more pronounced, the cheeks hollower, the skin sallow, dry and papery. He wore a blue linen shirt, neatly pressed trousers and a black leather jacket.

'It's called *The Transfer Agreement*, by Edwin Black.'

'Never heard of the agreement or the book.' David shrugged.

'No surprise,' said Solly. 'It's a little-known story about an agreement between the Nazis and Jewish organisations to allow Jews who wished to leave Germany to emigrate.'

'Really?' asked David in a tone of disbelief.

Solly nodded. 'It was an arrangement that allowed German Jews to go to Palestine, but they had to leave all but a small portion of their assets behind. What they did take had to be in the form of German goods.'

'That's outrageous,' growled David.

'Hear me out,' said Solly. 'In 1933, shortly after Hitler came to power, the Jewish Agency for Palestine and the German Zionist Federation cut a deal with the German Ministry of Economics. Ths became known as the Transfer Agreement, and it remained in effect until war broke out in 1939.'

'What were the terms?' David clutched his spoon as if he were preparing an attack.

'German Jews could emigrate to Palestine and keep at least some of the value of their German assets by converting them into German goods for the Yishuv.'

'Clever, but at what cost?'

'Think about it from Ben-Gurion's perspective,' replied Solly. 'Those were the early days of Nazi Germany – long before the Holocaust and five years before Kristallnacht. The Jewish Agency thought it would benefit all concerned. Ben-Gurion knew that Germany wasn't a good place for Jews and wanted to build the Yishuv – the Hebrew term for Jewish communities in British Palestine.'

'I know, I know,' David said dryly.

Solly shrugged. 'Anyway, Ben-Gurion thought that an influx of German Jews with their capital – in whatever form – would be a win-win proposition.'

'And I guess the Nazis wanted to get rid of German Jews…'

'And they also sought to undermine the worldwide anti-Nazi trade boycott that had started in 1933. Remember, this was the decade of the Great Depression,' Solly added.

'And the German economy was in bad shape,' David agreed.

'Oh yeah,' confirmed Solly. 'Unemployment was rising, and the Nazis needed to export goods to create more jobs. The boycott was preventing that, so they came up with a way of getting goods out of Germany and into Israel. They must have been laughing all the way to the bank.' His voice was hard, almost ugly.

David nodded, glancing at the rain-washed windows, his face solemn. 'So, it was Nazi policy to force out as many Jews as possible while confiscating as much of their wealth as they could get away with.' His eyes burned.

'Yes, but they were cunning,' Solly said. 'They offered the Jews a way out, so long as they took their wealth in the form of German goods, thus sidestepping the boycott.'

David drew in his breath sharply and asked, 'What did Jewish organisations think of dealing with the Nazis?'

Solly shrugged. 'Their attitude was mixed. The American Jewish Congress and the Jewish War Veterans didn't want a bar of it. They supported the trade boycott. But the American Jewish Committee and B'nai B'rith were opposed to the boycott.'

David gave a wry smile. 'Typical; two Jews, three opinions. But why were those groups opposed?'

Solly shrugged. 'They worried that the boycott would anger the Nazis and make the situation for the Jews in Germany even worse.'

'What about this…what's his name? Your author.'

'Edwin Black?'

'Yes. Who did he support, the boycott or the Transfer Agreement?'

David was watching Solly, his face thoughtful.

'Black thought the trade boycott was the correct course of action. He regarded those organisations supporting the Transfer Agreement as tools of the Third Reich. He also said that in 1933 it was possible a wider and more effective trade boycott of German goods would have toppled Hitler.'

'That's a pretty ambitious claim,' snorted David. 'So, which countries boycotted trade with Germany?'

'The boycott was particularly strong in the United States, France and Great Britain,' Solly said. 'But I agree. The boycott would have failed anyway. Much of Eastern Europe was dependent on trade with Germany. There's no way they would have joined.'

'So, what did your man have to say about the Transfer Agreement?' David said.

Solly hesitated, then said, 'Black claims the Transfer Agreement was responsible for establishing the State of Israel. But he's wrong there as well.'

'Why do you disagree?' David asked.

'Black argues that 60,000 German Jews settled in Palestine between 1933 and 1941 because of the Transfer Agreement. But David Yisraeli, who's also written on the Transfer Agreement, says 33,000 emigrants settled in Palestine between 1932 and 1937, and only 12,500 used the Transfer Agreement. Also, Black claims that about $100 million of capital assets of German Jews went into building the State of Israel. But others argue the amount was only around $40 million.'

'So, who was right?' David pressed.

Solly was silent for a moment. 'Not Black, I think,' he replied. 'As it turned out, the Agreement accounted for only 0.1 per cent of all German exports to Palestine.'

'So that means his argument that the Agreement contributed to the building of the Jewish state is quite a stretch,' David said, his eyes sharp.

Solly laughed. 'Black accuses the Zionist movement of destroying the trade boycott and thereby granting a reprieve to the Third Reich. But I don't think that's fair. Just because some Zionists supported the Transfer Agreement and not the trade boycott doesn't mean they gave the Nazis a leg-up. Ben-Gurion and the Yishuv had the best interests of the Jewish people at heart. Again, remember that the full horror of the Holocaust was still beyond everyone's worst imagining.'

'As you know, my family comes from Poland,' said David. 'What happened there? Did the Polish Jewish organisations support the trade boycott?'

'Some did,' Solly said. 'They agitated against the Nazis, promoting the boycott and prosecution of those who violated it.'

'Did those efforts work?' David looked at Solly quizzically.

Solly nodded. 'In 1932 German exports to Poland dropped from 173 million zloty to 146 million, and in 1934 to 108 million.'

'Good for them,' smiled David. 'How did the Nazis respond?'

Solly looked at David narrowly. 'Not well. The German Foreign Ministry sent a rabbi to Warsaw to convince Jewish businessmen to lift the boycott, but without success. The Polish Jews told him to go home.'

'And what about the German Jews?' David asked. Did they support the boycott?'

'Ah,' sighed Solly. 'Many German Jews opposed it for fear it would escalate antisemitism in Germany and worsen their economic situation.'

David was silent for a moment and then asked, 'So who else supported the boycott?'

'Ze'ev Jabotinsky, the leader of conservative Revisionist Zionism. He advocated for Jewish emigration from Poland and for maintaining the boycott.'

'What about the Yishuv?'

Solly took a sip of coffee then said, 'Opinions were mixed.'

'And what about other Eastern European countries?' asked David. 'What was their attitude to the boycott?'

'In 1933, Jewish businesses in Lithuanian and Romania boycotted German goods and there was also a lot of support among Eastern European Jews in the United States, who were committed to the boycott.'

'So, it spread pretty widely.' David smiled.

'And spontaneously.' Solly nodded. 'It went to show that many Jews were refusing to accept the Nazis' antisemitic policies, but support wasn't unanimous.'

'Back to the two Jews three opinions thing again?' asked David.

'Well, the Polish delegation to the World Jewish Congress in Geneva in 1933 said the Transfer Agreement infringed on Jewish dignity and weakened the struggle against Nazi Germany.'

David began to tug at his earlobe, absorbed in thought. 'So, what was the attitude of the Zionist movement?' he finally asked.

'Also conflicted,' Solly replied. 'On the one hand the Agreement supported the needs of the Yishuv, but many also sympathised with the sentiments of the Jewish people who supported the trade boycott. It was also political.'

'Isn't everything with our people?' David said.

Solly smiled before going on. 'Between 1931 and 1933, Labour Zionism and Jabotinsky's Revisionist Zionist Alliance were in a struggle for domination of the Yishuv. Mapai, the dominant labour party, found support within the Yishuv, while Jabotinsky and the Revisionists were supported by the Polish Jewish middle class.'

'How did that political fight play out?' David pressed.

'It happened at the Eighteenth Zionist Congress in Prague,' Solly explained. 'Ben-Gurion, the Mapai leader, and Jabotinsky, the Revisionist, campaigned vigorously against each other.'

'What was the outcome?'

'Labour Zionism won 138 out of 318 seats with 44 per cent of the votes cast. This strengthened Mapai's power in the Congress, which meant Labour members were elected to key positions in the Jewish Agency for Israel as well, which, as you know, was committed to establishing Israel as a Jewish homeland for the Jewish people and encouraging Jews to immigrate to Israel. Ben-Gurion became chairman of the Jewish Agency, Moshe Sharett was appointed head of its Political Department, and Eliezer Kaplan was made Treasurer. All Labour men. But the Histadrut was conflicted about the Agreement.'

'What was that?' asked David.

'The Histadrut is the trade union movement and is closely affiliated with Mapai. But it ducked the conflict between the

Transfer Agreement and the boycott until 1934, when it was pressured to take a stand on an agreement concerning the export of Jaffa oranges from Palestine. At that time, Germany was a big importer of citrus fruit, and that contract violated the worldwide Jewish boycott.' His voice was matter-of-fact.

'So, what happened?'

'The Histadrut's governing committee was divided between pro- and anti-boycott factions. In the end, five committee members voted for the orange export agreement with Germany, one abstained and one voted no. As you can imagine that decision was very controversial.'

'Oh yeah,' David muttered. 'I'm sure a lot of people were annoyed. It's a tough issue, and I imagine there were good arguments on both sides.'

'Hmm, sure. Anyway, at the Nineteenth Zionist Congress in September 1935, future Israeli prime minister Golda Meir spoke for Mapai in support of the Transfer Agreement. She argued that it would help to save thousands of Jewish lives.'

'I understand,' David said.

'But in the end the Zionist Congress endorsed the Transfer Agreement by a vote of 169 in favour, 12 opposed and 17 abstentions. By way of context, I think it's fair to say that Nazi rule in Germany at the time was still new. And Zionist consciousness at the time was shaped by the fate of Soviet Jews after the Bolshevik Revolution,' Solly said.

'In what way?' David asked.

Solly gave David a brief, tentative smile. 'Well, prior to the revolution, Russian Jewry was considered the core of European Jewry. But after 1918, the Jews of the Soviet Union grew apart from the rest of the Jewish people, and the Jewish centre in Europe shifted.'

David frowned. 'Is this because the Soviets banned the Jewish religion?' David asked.

'The communists were anti-religion in general,' said Solly. 'But they also placed strict immigration controls on all Soviet citizens. Some Jewish leaders warned that the Zionist movement should distance itself from the trade boycott for fear the Jews of Germany might suffer the same fate as Russian Jewry, and not be allowed to travel to Palestine.'

'I'm not sure I follow,' said David.

'Let me put it this way,' replied Solly, taking off his glasses. 'Some supported the Transfer Agreement because without it they believed German Jewry would be imprisoned like Russian Jewry was in the USSR. So anything that facilitated a dialogue between the Yishuv and Nazi Germany and allowed Jews to emigrate to Palestine offered a chance for deliverance that could not be missed. From this perspective, it's not surprising the Yishuv leadership opposed the boycott. They thought it might disrupt the opportunity for German Jews to emigrate.'

David sat quietly, a pensive expression on his face. 'I don't quite know what to think.'

'I get it,' nodded Solly. 'And remember, the Jewish boycott had little effect on the German economy. I think it was pretty naive on the part of world Jewish organisations to think that they could curtail, let alone overwhelm, Nazi Germany's economic capability.'

'I suppose so,' agreed David.

'And with the passage of time, the Jewish boycott against Nazi Germany slipped off the public agenda. Again, most of the world was focused on the Great Depression. And the German–Polish non-aggression treaty in 1935 weakened anti-Nazi initiatives in Poland. In fact, the Polish government even promised to act against the anti-German boycott committees in Poland.'

'How long did the Transfer Agreement remain in effect?' David asked quietly.

'On paper, until the war started in 1939, although difficulties in implementation emerged before that. It turned out that the fledgling economy of Mandatory Palestine was unable to absorb Jewish capital in the form of goods.'

'Then that was the end of it,' muttered David.

'Not quite,' said Solly, pausing for a sip of coffee. 'In March 1937, the Jewish agency concluded a similar deal with Poland. This one was called the Clearing Agreement, and its purpose was to enable Jewish emigrants from Poland to transfer their assets to Palestine by purchasing Polish goods. Unlike the Transfer Agreement, it enabled transfers of money as well as goods from Poland to Palestine and vice versa.'

'What did Jabotinsky and the Revisionists think about it?'

Solly laughed. 'They tried to cut their own deal with the Polish government to circumvent the Jewish Agency.'

David shook his head. 'Jewish politics!'

'Precisely,' nodded Solly. 'But the condition of Polish Jewry deteriorated over the 1930s and the Revisionists and Mapai began to cooperate with each other. Because Mapai and the Zionist Congress supported the Transfer Agreement, it's fair to say that this put the final nail in the coffin of the boycott movement.'

'So, it really was a deal with the devil,' David said as he picked up his muffin and took a bite.

'Yes, the Transfer Agreement won out,' Solly replied.

Outside, it began to hail. A cold wind blew into the café and the two men glanced around, shrugged, then reached for their cappuccinos.

Night of Broken Glass

'Dad,' Rita said, clearing her throat, 'how did my great-grandpa die? I know it wasn't a heart attack. I want to know the truth.'

She was leaning on the kitchen bench as I tried to concentrate on making the coffee, her jeans torn at the knees in current youthful fashion and the laces of her sneakers absent. I waited while the coffee-maker heated, then said quietly, 'Suicide.' I sighed.

Her face settled into a grim frown. 'I thought that might be it. Because of the Nazis?'

'It was Kristallnacht,' I said.

'That was an anti-Jewish riot, wasn't it? We learned about it at school.'

'Pogrom would be a better word. Between the 9th and 10th of November 1938 there was an orchestrated attack throughout Germany against Jewish homes, businesses and synagogues.'

'Orchestrated as in centrally planned?' she asked.

'Oh yes,' I nodded. 'The orders came straight from the top. The street thugs of the SA were the main foot soldiers of the pogrom. But SS troopers and German civilians took part as well.'

'And this caused Great-grandpa to kill himself?' she asked in a trembling voice as tears began to well in the corners of her eyes.

'Yes it did,' I sighed. 'And he wasn't the only one.'

'What do you mean?'

'I mean there were over 600 suicides among German Jews after Kristallnacht.'

Rita wiped her cheek and sniffed. 'So it was a preview of the Holocaust?'

'I would describe it as a milestone on the road to Auschwitz,' I replied. 'Before Hitler's rise to power, Jews were well integrated into German society. Of course there was antisemitism, but not enough to prevent Jews from playing a major role in business, science and culture. Over 100,000 Jews served in the German army during the First World War, with around 12,000 sacrificing their lives.'

'So when did it begin to go downhill?' Rita asked.

'There were sporadic acts of antisemitism after Hitler became chancellor in early 1933. But the big change came two years later with the enactment of the Nuremberg Laws. Those laws stripped German Jews of their citizenship. Their property was confiscated and many were thrown into the first concentration camp, at Dachau.'

'Monsters,' she muttered.

'Oh yes,' I agreed. 'Many Jews wanted to leave, but most countries had no desire to accept Jewish refugees.'

'More antisemitism.' Rita sighed.

'In part. But you also have to remember that this was the middle of the Great Depression. Millions of people were out of work and it would have been political suicide to allow in large numbers of refugees…regardless of who they might be.'

'I guess…' she said. 'Did any manage to get out?'

'Around 250,000 went to Palestine, but then the British shut off Jewish immigration through their White Paper of 1939.'

'The bastards,' Rita said.

'It was a bastard of a thing to do,' I nodded. 'But the British wanted to guarantee supplies of Arab oil for war with Germany, which by then they could see was inevitable.'

'And sacrificing the Jews was just the cost of doing business,' she sneered.

'The real irony was that this British attempt to placate the Arabs failed. Amin al-Husseyni spent the war in Berlin plotting with Heinrich Himmler how to export the Holocaust to the Middle East if Rommel won in North Africa.'

'Who was…Amin al-Husseyni?' Rita asked.

'The Grand Mufti of Jerusalem and leader of the Palestinian Arabs. Iraqis also mounted a pro-German uprising in 1941.'

'But what about Great-grandfather?'

'Right. Well, the death camps hadn't been built, but concentration camps were already fully operational. Jewish passports were marked with the letter J, phones were being tapped and the dragnet was closing in. My grandfather went from hiding place to hiding place in an attempt to escape the Gestapo.'

Knitting her eyebrows as she always did when she was curious, Rita enquired, 'Didn't he try to get away?'

'His sister, brother-in-law and brother fled to Vilnius, but Grandpa stayed because he couldn't bear to leave his parents. He thought things weren't as bad as all that and wouldn't get any worse. He believed that Nazi antisemitism couldn't last; he clung to the hope that they lived in a democracy, not a madhouse.'

'What about everyone else?' asked Rita. 'All the other Germans? Did they just stand by and watch?'

I shrugged. 'Do you mean on Kristallnacht? Some people gathered and watched in silence as the rioters burned synagogues… some centuries old. It went on throughout the night in full view of the public and of local firefighters, who had received orders to intervene only to prevent flames from spreading to nearby buildings. Fires were lit, and prayer books, scrolls, artworks and philosophy texts were thrown on the flames, and buildings were burned or vandalised.'

'It seems to have happened so quickly, it must have been an enormous shock,' Rita exclaimed.

'Members of the Hitler Youth threw bricks and shattered the shop windows of Jewish-owned businesses and department stores then looted them. There was no warning.'

'How terrifying,' Rita said, pushing back in her chair.

'Tombstones were uprooted and graves violated in Jewish cemeteries, and other sacred sites were desecrated.'

'Shocking,' Rita said.

'Mobs of SA men attacked Jews in their homes and ransacked their houses or roamed the streets attacking Jews, forcing them to perform acts of public humiliation. Police records indicate that not only were many Jewish lives lost that night, but also there were many assaults and suicides.'

'It is beyond comprehension how people could behave like that,' Rita said, taken aback.

'Children threw stones at the windows of Jewish shops and nobody intervened. It was anarchy. Jewish property, Jewish people, were ruthlessly attacked.

Rita looked at me but remained silent. It was as if she couldn't find the words to express her shock and anger.

'My family had seen several anti-Jewish outbursts in Germany during the preceding years, but nothing as bad as that.'

'I don't doubt it.'

'It was as if normal people, civilised people, became barbarians, filled with antisemitism and blood lust. Synagogues throughout Germany and Austria were set alight. Siddur prayer books and Torah scrolls were cast onto bonfires. Mobs of Nazi hooligans roamed the streets looting, raping and murdering.'

Rita blanched. 'There…there were rapes?'

'Yes,' I snorted. 'Hundreds of them. Never mind the Nuremberg Laws against sexual relations between Jews and Aryans. And there were women cheering on the mob while mothers held up their children to see the fun.'

'It makes me so angry,' Rita hissed.

It's almost enough to make you glad for every bomb dropped by the RAF and Americans on German cities…almost. You never met Aunty Esther. I hate to say it, but she was violated by the Nazis.'

'How shocking!'

'She never spoke about it, but she carried the scars.'

'I don't wonder.' Rita indicated for me to continue.

'Very few people dared protest in public.'

'Pathetic,' Rita said. 'They should have shown some spine and stood up against the Nazi regime.'

'Easy to say now,' I sighed. 'But are you certain you'd have that sort of courage?'

Rita glared at me.

'Anyway, Goebbels explained away the burned synagogues and looted Jewish property as a spontaneous expression of indignation against the murder of a German diplomat in Paris.'

Rita listened to me in silence, her eyes closed.

I turned my attention to the coffee and set out two cups.

'One time, my grandfather received a telephone call from a business acquaintance warning that Jews were about to be arrested.'

'"There must be a mistake," Grandpa protested. "No mistake," said the acquaintance. "I called to warn you." But Grandpa wouldn't believe it could be true.'

'So what convinced him?' Rita asked.

'My grandmother, Sara, insisted they leave.'

'How do you know all this?'

'Your great-aunt, Esther,' I said. 'She told me the story. She was one of the lucky ones who emerged from the war with her life.'

'Hardly lucky given what happened to her,' Rita said sharply.

'Of course. But she lived. She had years of life after the war, until cancer killed her. Now, let me concentrate on this coffee.' I busied myself with the milk frothing and coffee and handed her a cup.

'Thanks,' she said. 'So how did your grandfather and his family escape?' Rita pressed.

'The story goes that on the second night, the 10th of November, the doorbell rang and then fists began pounding on the door. A crowd outside began demanding entry, yelling "Open up, Jew, open up!" Your great-grandfather grabbed the Webley revolver he'd brought back from the war…' I took a sip of coffee.

'What happened?' Rita demanded.

'He was a fighter,' I said. 'But as luck would have it, Ernst Hartman, his gentile business partner, happened to be visiting that night. He volunteered to answer the front door while the family went out the back. As they slipped out the back door, Grandpa heard his friend arguing with the stormtroopers.'

Rita sat forward on the edge of her seat. 'What did he hear?'

'Apparently, his business partner declared on his honour as a member of the Nazi Party that there were no Jews in the house.'

'Was he?'

'A party member?' I shrugged. 'I don't know. But I do know that Ernst Hartman showed himself to be a decent person that night. And he suffered for it.'

'What do you mean?' Rita asked.

'One of the SA stormtroopers yelled, "Don't mix with Jews", and kicked Hartman in the groin.'

'That's terrible!' she cried.

'The next day your great-grandfather bought a newspaper. The headlines read "The Murder in Paris", and "Jews Declare War on the German People", and other such nonsense.'

'What utter bulldust!' spat Rita.

'Of course. The Nazis were capitalising on the actions of Herschel Grynszpan.'

'Who was he?' she asked.

'He was a Jew living illegally in France. Despite being born in Hanover, he was not a German citizen. Nor were his parents. When his mother and father were expelled across the border into Poland in October 1938, Grynszpan swore revenge. He bought a pistol and walked into the German embassy in Paris. He shot the first official he saw, a junior diplomat named Ernst vom Rath, who died a few days later.'

'And that was the excuse the Nazis needed?' Rita asked.

'Precisely,' I said. 'Hitler used vom Rath's death as a pretext for the Kristallnacht pogrom. There are those who say the murder was the result of a homosexual love affair gone wrong. But I don't believe it.'

Rita's brow rose in a quizzical arch. 'Why not?'

'I think it was a tactic Grynszpan was planning to use to embarrass the Nazis at his trial.'

'So he was extradited to Germany?'

I shook my head. 'No, he was initially prosecuted and imprisoned in Paris. But the Germans got hold of him in 1940, after the surrender of France. Historians found correspondence from the Reich Justice Ministry warning about Grynszpan's plan to use the jilted gay lover defence.'

'So what happened?' asked Rita.

'The trial never took place. Grynszpan remained in prison at SS headquarters in Berlin and there's considerable controversy about his fate.'

'What do you mean?'

'Some argue that he was murdered in his cell, while others claim Grynszpan was seen in Paris after the war. But I don't know.'

'So what happened to the Jews after Kristallnacht?' Rita asked.

'The next day, Jewish children were expelled from state elementary schools. Jewish newspapers were shut down and cultural activities outlawed. Any Jew caught with a firearm was subject to twenty years' imprisonment.'

'So the Jews were disarmed and helpless with no ability to resist.'

'Pretty much,' I acknowledged. 'All in all, over 30,000 Jewish men were sent to concentration camps like Dachau and Buchenwald. More than 250 synagogues were destroyed throughout the Reich.'

'Terrible,' said Rita, 'but mild compared to what came later, I guess.'

I took my coffee around the bench to the stool and perched there, reaching for the biscuit jar. I offered her first choice.

'Thanks,' she said, taking two chocolate-coated ones.

'Towards the end of her life, Aunt Esther would lie in bed beneath heavy blankets talking about life in the "*alte land*" – that's old country in Yiddish. She would smile as she spoke about her comfortable life in Berlin during the 1920s. But when she moved on to life under Hitler, her tears would begin to flow.'

Rita leant over the bench and kissed me on the forehead. 'I'm sorry, Papa.'

'Anyway, Kristallnacht triggered one last wave of Jewish emigration from Germany. Most went to other European countries like Holland and France.'

Rita sighed. 'Which means they were once again in danger after those countries fell to the Germans.'

'Yes,' I answered, 'but some were able to reach Palestine and a handful gained visas for the US. Several thousand more fled to Shanghai, where they were left alone by the Japanese army after war broke out in December 1941.'

'And your grandfather?' Rita asked in a subdued voice, 'Why did he suicide?'

'My grandfather…your great-grandfather…was not a well man. He had terrible health problems. Add Nazi antisemitism to the mix and you have a recipe for hell on earth. It was hard for Jews unless they had a lot of money hidden away.'

'So sad,' Rita murmured.

'That it was,' I nodded. 'Little by little he had to sell his property, first the warehouses, then the block of flats, and the apartment. According to Esther, he couldn't bear to tell his family the truth. My grandmother was still buying new clothes and expensive crystalware. But the bills kept mounting. He managed to buy my father a ticket to Australia – he couldn't afford to pay for my uncle's college tuition or my aunt's wedding dress. By the end, he couldn't even pay the butcher or the rent when it was collected in the courtyard where he had once sat as the owner.'

I paused and pulled a tissue from a box on the bench to wipe the tears away. 'I guess he just couldn't bear it any longer.' I sighed.

'It was like that, in those days. People watched their lives slipping away as they lost their social position and were unable to support their families. So many Jewish men just came home one day and killed themselves.'

Rita was silent.

Taking a deep breath, I went on. 'It's strange, really. Later, in the ghetto, people didn't often kill themselves. It was mostly the opposite. People wanted to hang on to life just one more day in the hope of seeing the Germans lose the war before they died. But my grandfather never saw any of that. And if he'd known what he left them behind to face, I'm sure he would never have done it.'

I glanced up and saw the pain etched across Rita's face. 'Do you want to stop?'

She shook her head. But I still didn't know what to do. Should I continue to talk? Or would I just upset her more? I recalled the tears rolling down Esther's old, lined cheeks when she was lying in bed, and she told me my grandfather had hanged himself. But other people said he jumped from a window. In things like that, people don't always want to share the details. But the story itself always ended the same…with my grandfather dead.

'Was there any dissent among the Nazi leadership?' Rita suddenly asked.

'Not really,' I shrugged. 'Göring was slightly annoyed because he wanted to steal Jewish property intact, rather than destroy it. He met with other members of the Nazi leadership a couple of days later and introduced a letter from the Führer requesting that the Jewish question be solved. So he canvassed the meeting for ideas about how best to eliminate the Jewish presence once and for all from the German economy.'

'Monsters,' Rita said. 'Gluttonous monsters.'

'Oh, yes indeed,' I said. 'Of course, you've heard about Göring's collection of plundered art?'

Rita nodded.

'Anyway, the persecution inflicted on German Jews continued after Kristallnacht. The community was forced to pay a levy of twenty per cent on all Jewish property for the murder of vom Rath. A fine of another six million Reichsmarks was imposed for property damage to the Reich government, for damages to the German nation, and Jews were required to pay for the damage caused by the pogrom to their residences and businesses.'

'Those freaks,' fumed Rita. 'What about the world? Didn't they see what was happening?'

'In a way, Kristallnacht was the moment the world became aware of the extent of antisemitism in Nazi Germany. The pogrom was too vast and brutal to conceal. And Goebbels's rationalisations and justifications rang hollow to the international community and the rest of the world. The Nazi government's deliberate policy of inciting violence laid bare the repressive nature and widespread antisemitism entrenched in Germany.'

Rita leaned back. 'But to what effect?'

'World opinion on the Nazis soured. Regrettably, here in Australia, it was only an Indigenous leader named William Cooper who led a march through the streets of Melbourne to the German Consulate where he delivered a petition condemning the persecution of the Jews. German officials refused to accept the petition.'

'That's amazing!' marvelled Rita.

'William Cooper was a voice of righteousness in a wilderness of indifference. But it's also true that many newspapers began to condemn the Third Reich. *The Times* of London called Kristallnacht a disgrace.'

'An understatement,' sighed Rita, 'but better than nothing, I suppose.'

The Americans recalled their ambassador from Berlin, but stopped short of severing diplomatic relations.'

'Typical of the Yanks,' snorted Rita.

'Well, Winston Churchill did once say that the Americans always did the right thing…after trying every possible alternative.'

Rita couldn't contain a grim smile at Churchill's witticism.

'In Britain, the Chamberlain government agreed to receive one thousand German Jewish children…the so-called Kindertransport.'

'One thousand…'

We were both silent for a time. Then Rita said, 'So it's fair to say that Kristallnacht was a prelude to the Holocaust.'

I nodded. 'It ramped up Nazi persecution of the Jews from economic and social exclusion to brute violence. Kristallnacht was a foreshadowing of Babi Yar and Auschwitz.'

Finding Home

'When Dad told me that we were leaving Germany to take a ship to the other side of the world, I struggled to understand what that meant.' Abe smiled at his grandson Joshua.

They were sitting in the study of Abe's home in the wealthy suburb of Toorak. Two walls were covered with bookshelves filled with fiction and historical works, all of them sorted in alphabetical order. A third wall of windows overlooked a plush green courtyard full of magnolias, Japanese maples and azaleas, and the fourth was covered with Bergner oil paintings from his Holocaust series.

'It was exciting to be going on a luxury liner, but I was scared,' Abe said, his eyes widening in reminiscence. 'We didn't really know where we were going, or how we'd cope when we got there. All we knew was that we had to get out of Germany.'

'How old were you?' Joshua asked, his voice cracking to a high, thin child's pitch. Joshua wore a rumpled white shirt, tan shorts and an old pair of runners with the laces untied. His wild brown hair needed trimming and his blue eyes peered out through black-rimmed glasses that were too large for his narrow face.

'I was twelve. And still today, at ninety, I can remember the thrill of boarding a luxury liner, the *St Louis*, at Hamburg, combined with fear of the unknown. My mother was concerned about taking such a long journey by herself with me and my sister. I can still see her anxious frown, and the way she gnawed at her lip.'

'But you had to get away from the Nazis, right?' Joshua asked, his eyebrows arched.

'In the years following the rise of Hitler in 1933, ordinary Jewish families like ours had no doubt about the increasing dangers we were facing. Jewish properties were being confiscated, synagogues and businesses burned down. And then there was Kristallnacht in November 1938. My father was a Polish citizen. When he was deported from Wandsbek back to Poland my mother decided it was time to leave.'

'I never knew I had a Polish great-grandfather,' Joshua said quietly.

'It was a terrible time. After Kristallnacht the Germans argued that the unwillingness of other nations to admit Jewish refugees justified their antisemitic policies.' I sighed. 'The past still haunts me.'

'How could it not?' Joshua said, leaning over and patting the papery skin of his grandfather's hand.

'And yet, for much of my adulthood I thought my survival depended on keeping the past and its darkness locked away. I hid from the past because I feared I'd be swallowed up by it all. So, I worked hard to keep that pain buried. But by choosing not to face the past I realised I was choosing not to be free. I had my secret, and my secret had me.'

'What do you mean, your secret had you, *Zayde*?'

'Let me put it another way. I realised that when we force our truths into hiding, secrets become their own trauma, their own prison. Far from diminishing pain, if we deny ourselves the opportunity to accept past trauma, it becomes inescapable. Freedom lies in learning to embrace what has happened. It means we must muster the courage to dismantle the prison, brick by brick. Do you see what I mean?'

'I think so,' the boy said.

'There's a difference between victimisation and victimhood. Victimisation comes from the outside. From a bully, for example. By contrast, victimhood comes from the inside. No one can make you a victim but you. We become victims not because of what happens to us, but how we respond to misfortune or evil. It makes us into our own jailors when we choose the confines of the victim's mind.'

'Yes, I can see now,' Joshua said. 'So what happened after Kristallnacht?'

'We lived in fear for six months, and then my mother had had enough. She decided we were leaving. Apparently my father pleaded with her to wait until he could get back to Germany from Poland. But my mother insisted on going.'

'She did the right thing,' smiled Joshua.

'She tried to,' Abe nodded. 'I have an image of my father, as I had known him my entire life, cigarette hanging out of his mouth, tape measure around his neck, chalk in his hand for marking a pattern onto expensive cloth, his eyes twinkling, ready to burst into song, about to tell a joke…'

A smile spread across Joshua's face.

'He wanted to be a lawyer, not a tailor. But that was a dream his father discouraged. Every once in a while he would express his disappointment.'

Joshua studied his grandfather's face for a moment. 'It must have been difficult to leave without him.'

'Very,' sighed Abe. 'The day we left I felt as though I would vomit. I'm sure my mother felt dreadful too, but she believed we had to go. So with those visas for Cuba she had bought in Berlin, ten German marks in her purse and another 200 hidden in her underclothes, we headed for Hamburg.'

'You and your sister were lucky that your mother had such foresight and courage,' smiled Joshua, pride evident in his voice.

Abe nodded. 'The whole family came down to the *bahnhof* – the railway station – in Berlin to see us off. We were all afraid that we'd never see each other again.'

'You were fortunate,' said Joshua. 'You managed to get out.'

'But I never did see any of them again.' Abe sniffled. 'Over twenty aunts, uncles and cousins. All gone. And we were such a close family.'

Abe shut his eyes and leaned back in his chair. 'I still miss them terribly.'

'What about the voyage?' Joshua asked, to distract his grandfather.

'As I said, we left Hamburg for Havana, Cuba, on the 13th of May 1939. We were lucky. We were three of the 937 passengers on board. Most were Jews fleeing from the Nazis. The plan was to stay in Cuba until we could enter the United States.'

'So, when you boarded the boat you must have felt safe at last,' Joshua said.

'We found out later that the ship's owners thought we might have trouble disembarking in Cuba,' Abe said.

'And they kept it a secret?' Joshua asked, adjusted the yarmulka on his head.

'We knew nothing about it. As the coast of Germany disappeared over the horizon, we thought we were safe.'

'But you weren't?'

'We weren't,' sighed Abe. 'The US State Department, Jewish organisations and refugee agencies were all aware of the problem once we arrived in Cuba, but we, the passengers, were kept in the dark. We held landing certificates and transit visas, so we thought we were safe. We didn't know that the Cuban President, Federico Laredo Brú, had issued a decree before the ship sailed that invalidated the landing certificates.'

'What? Why?' asked Joshua.

'We didn't know it at the time, but before the ship sailed there was a bitter battle within the Cuban government.' Abe closed his eyes and leaned his head back against the chair. 'Turns out the conservative Cuban press demanded that the government stop admitting Jewish refugees.'

'But why?' Joshua asked with a frown.

'You have to remember that the 1930s was the decade of the Great Depression. Cuba was struggling economically and many people resented the Jews the government had already admitted into the country. There were over two thousand of them.'

'Because of jobs?'

'Smart boy,' smiled Abe. 'Because they competed for scarce jobs.'

'So, it wasn't antisemitism?' asked Joshua.

Abe shook his head. 'The real world isn't that simple. Even before the *St Louis* sailed there was an antisemitic demonstration in Havana with 40,000 people. A one-time president of Cuba apparently said, "Fight the Jews until the last one is driven out."'

'Fools,' Joshua muttered.

A cold breeze lifted the curtains.

'*Shver tsu zayn a Yid*,' sighed Abe.

'I know that one…"it's hard to be a Jew" – Yiddish, yes?'

'That's right. Still today we encounter prejudice, subtle and explicit. Remember, antisemitism wasn't a Nazi invention. It's been around for thousands of years. Growing up, I believed it was safer not to admit I was Jewish, that it was better to assimilate, to blend in, to never stand out. It was difficult to find a sense of identity and belonging.'

'I'm sorry, *Zayde*,' sighed Joshua.

'Not your fault, *bubbe*,' Abe replied. 'Anyway, the director-general of the Cuban immigration office was accused of selling landing certificates. He racked up a personal fortune of between half a million and a million dollars, and when the scandal broke he resigned in disgrace.'

'Was Cuba your only choice?'

'More or less. By early 1939, most countries had imposed quotas limiting the number of Jewish refugees. Palestine was not an option because the British were about to pass the White Paper blocking Jewish immigration. So, we saw Cuba as a temporary transit point on the way to America. And officials at the Cuban embassy in Berlin were selling visas for about \$200 or \$300 each. That's about \$3,000 to \$5,000 at today's prices.'

'How was the voyage?' Joshua asked.

'For many of us younger passengers, and our mother I think, the apprehension and anxiety soon faded as the coast of Europe disappeared over the horizon.'

'How did you spend your time?'

'I shared a cabin in the lower part of the ship with my sister, your aunty Rita. There was a girl named Anna who noticed me one day. I saw her looking at me every time I came to dinner. She was my age with wavy red hair and freckles. She smelt so good, like fresh air. Eventually I plucked up courage to speak to her. Each morning I looked forward to spending my time with her. We'd walk around the deck together holding hands, chatting and occasionally swimming in the ship's pool. Our relationship meant everything to me.'

'That sounds nice,' smiled Joshua.

'It was. In the darkness and chaos of uncertainty, Anna and I provided light for each other. Each day we talked about our future. There was a dance band and a cinema where the adults went when we kids were in bed. And we ate a variety of food that we rarely saw back home.'

'So, you were treated well?'

'Under orders from the ship's captain, Gustav Schröder, the waiters and crew treated us politely. It was a stark contrast to the open hostility we'd become accustomed to under the Nazis. He even allowed Shabbat prayers to be held – and you know what?'

'What, Grandpa,' Joshua asked, his face expectant.

'He gave permission for the portrait of Adolf Hitler hanging in the main dining room to be taken down during services.'

'Wow,' Joshua marvelled. 'He sounds like he was a decent man.'

Abe nodded. 'Everyone seemed so happy. We kids were told by our parents that we were now safe from harm. I heard people say, "We don't have to look over our shoulders anymore."'

'So, what happened when you got to Cuba?'

Abe grimaced. 'When we reached Havana on the 27th of May, I was on deck with my sister and mother with suitcases packed and ready to disembark. But when the Cuban officials, all smiles, first came aboard, it became clear that we weren't going to dock and wouldn't be allowed to disembark. I kept hearing the words *mañana, mañana* – tomorrow, tomorrow.'

'And then what?' asked Joshua.

'After the Cubans left, the ship's captain announced that we'd have to wait. That's when I knew something was wrong. I felt numb. Water carts were delivered to the ship and in the heat people began pushing and shoving to scoop a pail of it.'

'That sounds awful,' said Joshua.

'Ultimately, the Cubans admitted twenty-eight passengers who had US visas or were valid third-country passengers. As for the rest of us, an American attorney named Lawrence Berenson met with the Cuban President Brú to try and negotiate additional entry permits. But Brú refused and ordered the ship to leave Cuban territorial waters. So, the *St Louis* sailed north toward Miami.'

'What a heartless thing to do!'

'If my memory serves me correctly, one other passenger was evacuated to a hospital in Havana after attempting suicide. But the Cuban government refused to admit anyone else.'

'So, what did you do?'

'It became a big news story. Even though the US newspapers were sympathetic to our plight, only a few journalists took the risk of suggesting we be admitted to America. When we arrived off the coast of Florida, US authorities also refused us the right to dock. Captain Schröder had no option but to turn back towards Europe. We were crushed.'

Joshua shook his head. 'I can't imagine…'

'A pall settled over all of us. As the ship headed north-east across the Atlantic, I kept asking my mother whether we were going back to see our grandparents. My mother just shook her head in silent despair. People wandered about the ship in tears. One man even slit his wrists and threw himself overboard. If I close my eyes, I can still hear his shrieks and see the blood.'

Joshua's eyes filled with tears and he swiped at them with the back of one hand.

'The worst part was that we were sailing so close to the Florida coast we could see the lights of Miami. Some passengers cabled President Franklin D. Roosevelt asking for refuge, but he never responded.'

'Really?'

'No,' sighed Abe. 'The American government decided to refuse us entry. A State Department telegram they sent to us said we'd all have to wait our turn in the immigration queue for visas.'

'I thought Roosevelt was a friend of the Jews,' said Joshua. 'Why was he being so mean?'

Abe shrugged. 'America was still in an economic depression. Unemployment was around 17 per cent.'

'Is that high?'

'Very,' nodded Abe. 'Anything above 5 per cent is not great.'

'So, allowing immigrants into the country would have been unpopular,' Joshua mused.

'One magazine poll put popular opposition to immigration at over 80 per cent. Antisemitism was also very high in America at the time. There was a Catholic priest named Father Coughlin who had a radio show that was broadcast throughout the country. He used to read portions of the *Protocols of the Elders of Zion* on air to millions of his listeners.'

'Protocols of who?' Joshua asked, puzzled.

'It's an antisemitic fiction that claims there's a worldwide conspiracy amongst Jews to dominate the world.'

Joshua snorted. 'I can't believe it!'

'Believe it,' Abe sighed. 'America had a quota system that allocated visas by country. The annual quota for Germany was around 25,000, as I recall. It was filled several times over. There was a waiting list of several years. So, there was no hope for us. Roosevelt was too smart a politician to do something so unpopular.'

'Shocking!' said Joshua.

'It was what it was,' shrugged Abe. 'Earlier that year, Congress killed a bill that would have enabled 20,000 Jewish children to enter America over and above the quota.'

'Not even children?' asked Joshua.

Abe's shoulders heaved in another shrug. 'It wasn't only us. Two other ships carrying Jewish refugees sailed to Cuba around the same time. Like us, they were not permitted to dock. One sailed back to France while the other managed to finally unload its passengers in the Panama Canal Zone, which was governed back then by the US. Most of them eventually made it to America.'

'What about you? Did you end up back in Germany?'

'Thankfully not. After an American Jewish relief organisation put up a cash guarantee of half a million dollars, Belgium, the Netherlands, France and Britain each agreed to accept passengers. Anna's family and mine were the lucky ones who made it to the UK.'

'But the Germans later conquered France, Belgium and Holland,' said Joshua. 'What happened to the people who settled there?'

'After May 1940, they were in trouble,' said Abe. 'Some of them ran and some went into hiding. Only about half survived the war.'

'Wow, what a story!'

'And, as they say, the rest is history. As you know, Anna and I eventually married, had two sons and you are one of our five grandchildren.'

'At least something good came out of that whole mess,' said Joshua.

Abe smiled.

The Good Brother

'Why the smile?' Sophie asked. She was wearing denim jeans, fashionably torn at the knees, a beige silk blouse and black leather jacket. She looked gorgeous.

I shrugged. 'I just love this place. Great food and a super view of the Tan.' What I didn't say was that I'd be happy just about anywhere in her company. I glanced through the window and across Domain Road. The afternoon sun cast dancing shadows through the autumn leaves in the Royal Botanical Gardens.

'So, what's all this about Albert Göring?' Sophie asked as she sipped her pinot noir.

'You remember that conversation in the faculty lounge the first time we met?'

Sophie nodded. 'I mostly remember you, to tell the truth, and you're just as lovely today.'

'Stop it!' I blushed. 'I meant the conversation about our parents, and their influence on our work. I remember you said you wrote your thesis on the '68 Paris riots partly because of your family background.'

'That's right. And…?'

'I don't think I ever told you about my granddad.'

Sophie shook her head.

'He fought as a partisan with the Bielski brothers in Poland during the war.'

'That's amazing! I loved that movie with Daniel Craig…'

'*Defiance*,' I volunteered.

'Yeah…*Defiance*,' she echoed. 'So, he was a hero!'

I shrugged. 'It was…complicated.'

Her brow furrowed. 'How so?'

'The rest of his family…parents and three sisters…were all shot by the German *Ordnungspolizei*…the Order Police.'

'Like in Christopher Browning's *Ordinary Men*?' she asked, her face darkening.

I nodded.

'So, he was the only one to survive the war?'

'He survived in the physical sense.' I sighed. 'But mentally… that's another story. He lived with us, and there were days when he was unable to get out of bed because of his depression, and other times, for no apparent reason, he would lose his temper over the smallest things.

'He never spoke about his war experiences, and we knew never to mention that time of his life, but it was always there. The Holocaust has been a constant part of my entire life.'

'It must have been hard for you and your parents.'

I grimaced, trying to hold back sudden tears. 'The unpredictable outbursts were bad, but the most difficult thing was his inability to show any positive emotion. I don't think he ever told me he loved me, or anyone else for that matter.'

Sophie placed her hand over mine. At that moment she struck me as the most compassionate person I'd ever met. It was one of the reasons I adored her.

'Is that why you decided to do your doctorate on the Holocaust?' she asked.

'Actually, it was the idea of my honours thesis adviser. She suggested that I use my fluency in German to scour the archives and find a Holocaust-related issue that no one had written about. I remembered a journal article about Hermann Göring's brother who was anti-Nazi. She – my adviser – thought it was a great idea.'

Sophie shook her head. 'Wow. You mean to tell me that Hermann Göring had an anti-Nazi brother?'

'Yes, he did,' I replied. 'Hermann was the elder, by two years, and the second-most powerful man in the Third Reich. While he was giving orders to murder Jews, his younger brother Albert devoted himself to their salvation. It's an amazing story that hasn't really received the recognition it deserves.'

'But…but how did he survive? Did Hermann protect him?'

'That was part of it,' I said, 'but I think the Nazi hierarchy also turned a blind eye out of a desire to avoid the embarrassment of such a high-profile arrest.'

Sophie pondered this for several moments in silence. 'So, he was kind of another Oscar Schindler?'

I nodded. 'But Thomas Keneally didn't write a book about him.'

'But your doctoral thesis will provide some of that long-overdue recognition?'

'Yes, and I hope it provides a teaching position somewhere.' I grinned.

'Tell me about him, Albert I mean,' she prompted, putting down her glass.

'Well, Albert moved to Vienna after the Nazis came to power in Germany, which was fine until the Anschluss of '38.'

'Because…?'

'Because the Anschluss was the German annexation of Austria.'

'Of course.'

'I suppose you could say that he fled the Nazis, but the Nazis followed. He worked in the film industry and counted Jews among his closest friends.'

'How do you know so much about him if historians have ignored him?'

'Serendipity mostly,' I replied. 'I took a semester off between my second and third years at uni and travelled through Central and Eastern Europe. I wanted to see the sights…and visit the shtetl where my grandpa lived.'

'Which shtetl?'

'A place called Volozhyn. At the time it was part of Poland, but now it's in Belarus. However, my interest in Albert Göring was piqued in Prague, a city I love.'

'Prague?' Sophie echoed.

'A wonderful city,' I sighed. 'During the war Albert worked at the Skoda arms factory in Pilsen, which is only an hour or so out of Prague. While his factory was churning out weapons for the German army, he was utilising his position to save as many Jews as he could.'

'Amazing,' marvelled Sophie.

'It is remarkable,' I agreed. 'And I made an unsuccessful pilgrimage to try and find his grave on the outskirts of Munich. To pay my respects.'

'Nice,' smiled Sophie. 'But tell me more about him.'

'His father, Heinrich Göring, was a senior imperial diplomat who served as governor of German South West Africa during the 1880s. Hermann and Albert were born to Heinrich's second wife, Franziska Tiefenbrunn. They had a half-brother and two half-sisters from their father's first marriage. That second marriage was quite the scandal because she came from a peasant background.'

'Was Albert close to Hermann?'

'I think so,' I replied. 'Hermann was his elder brother. But having said that, while on trial at Nuremberg, Hermann described Albert as his antithesis.'

'In what way?'

'By all accounts, Hermann was a defiant child. He was transferred from school to school and at one of those schools he severed the strings of every violin and cello in the school orchestra, before taking off to avoid the consequences. His father finally sent him to military school, where he thrived.'

'And Albert?'

'He was more of an introvert who preferred reading to rough-housing. Unlike his brother, he had no interest in politics. He viewed the racial policies of the Nazi Party with disgust.'

'But I wonder why he chose such a different path,' Sophie said.

'There are all sorts of theories,' I replied. 'Their father, Heinrich, was away from the family on diplomatic missions for extended periods. Some people think that Albert was really the son of the family physician, who was a Jew.'

'What?' exclaimed Sophie.

'Yeah. The story goes that Fanny became infatuated with Doctor Hermann von Epenstein, a Jewish convert to Catholicism. During Heinrich's many absences, von Epenstein acted as a surrogate father to the Göring children. Some people think he might have been more.'

'More?' echoed Sophie.

I nodded. 'There are those who think Epenstein was Albert's biological father. There was a strong physical resemblance and Fanny brought the kids to live at Epenstein's Bavarian castle near Nuremburg.'

'Very Ramsay Street, German-style,' Sophie muttered.

I laughed. 'Yeah, they were more than neighbours. In 2016, Albert's daughter Elizabeth told the BBC that her mother confided that Albert had confessed to being Epenstein's son. He and Hermann shared the same mother, Fanny Göring, which would make Albert Hermann Göring's half-brother.'

'And with Jewish blood,' she said, glancing up at me.

'Indeed,' I smiled. 'Rather ironic, if true.'

Sophie nodded in agreement.

'In summer the Göring family lived in another one of Epenstein's castles, Burg Mauterndorf, in Salzburg. Everything was inspired by German romanticism and nationalism, with hunting horns calling diners to the table, servants dressed in medieval garb, and even minstrels, as if they were living in the Middle Ages.'

'Decadent,' she quipped, and we both began to laugh.

'World War I set them on sharply different paths. Hermann became a famous fighter ace, while Albert served in the signal corps. In 1919, Albert enrolled at the Technical University of Munich where he earned a degree in mechanical engineering. Coincidentally, Heinrich Himmler studied agronomy there.'

'Did they ever meet?' asked Sophie.

I shook my head. 'There's no evidence of a meeting. There were thousands of students on campus.'

'An interesting coincidence, nonetheless.'

I shrugged. 'By this time Albert had transformed himself from a shy bookish child to a bon vivant and ladies' man. He landed a job in Vienna and went through two marriages. He enjoyed Viennese culture – the wine, the social life – and he had a wide circle of Jewish friends, including two brothers, Oskar and Kurt Pilzer, who were part owners of a Viennese film company.'

'So, Albert thrived after the war?' Sophie asked.

'Oh yeah,' I confirmed, 'by comparison with Hermann, who bitterly resented his loss of status from war hero to unemployed veteran. He hated the reparations imposed on Germany by the Treaty of Versailles and gravitated toward a political activist named…'

'Adolf Hitler.'

'Precisely. By 1923, Hermann was one of Hitler's chief lieutenants and participated in the so-called Beer Hall Putsch.'

'What was that?'

'It was an attempted armed coup, during which Hermann Göring was shot,' I said. 'He took one to the groin.'

'Couldn't have happened to a nicer fellow,' said Sophie. 'If only that had been the end of him…'

'If only, and it almost was. The bullet had ricocheted of the muddy ground and started a serious infection. Hermann was cared for by two Jewish women who probably saved his life.'

'What a bitter irony,' Sophie said.

I was distracted by her mouth as she spoke. The other night she came back to my house, and we lay on my bed and talked. I'd leaned over to kiss her, but then hesitated. Did I dare go further? I wanted to, but was afraid of spoiling things. Unsure what to do, I began to massage her shoulders. After a while she rolled over and I worked on her back.

She was enjoying it and that had tempted me, but I decided to play it safe. Better to take it slow.

'Ahem,' Sophie cleared her throat.

'Sorry,' I shrugged. 'I was daydreaming about…well, you know.'

'Stay on track,' she grinned. 'There'll be time enough for more of that. Besides, Nazis and making out shouldn't mix.'

'Point taken,' I grinned back. 'So, anyway, Hermann became a morphine addict and was institutionalised in Sweden for a time.'

'So he was a drug addict in addition to being a Nazi mass-murderer?!'

'Yep,' I confirmed. 'And Hermann's descent into drugs marked the beginning of a twelve-year estrangement between the two brothers. It got worse when he joined up with Hitler; Albert viewed the Nazis with disgust and felt that Hermann's association with them brought shame to the family. But that's enough about me and my thesis. What about you? You've been to Europe? Tell me about it.'

Sophie smiled. 'Yes, several times. I love Italy in particular. And France of course, although my love of France is more… complicated.'

'Oh, what's your favourite city?' I asked.

'Venice…I love Venice.'

I shook my head. 'Too touristy.'

'You just haven't been there during the off-season,' Sophie said. 'In October the weather isn't too bad and there are usually no loud Americans to be seen, or heard.'

'Then maybe, one day, we should get tickets.' I grinned.

'Hold on there, cowgirl,' laughed Sophie, raising her palms. 'Tell me more about the Görings.'

'Really? Okay then. Well, as Hermann was rising through the ranks of the Nazi Party, Albert was trying to become a filmmaker in Vienna. He was also working to acquire emigration visas for his Jewish friends and acquaintances. By the time the Nazis annexed Austria in 1938, Albert was exhausted. But he agreed to meet his brother for the first time in twelve years.'

Sophie reached over and put her hand on mine. I paused, then muttered, 'I'm sorry.'

She smiled, took a sip of her pinot, and said, 'Sorry for what?'

'For blathering on ad nauseam. I can get carried away sometimes. We were talking about you.'

She shrugged. 'Well, you already know many things about me. You know I'm from Sydney. And that I majored in history there before coming to Melbourne for postgraduate study on the '68 riots in Paris…'

I smiled. 'Not ancient history.'

Sophie glanced at me with a shy smile. 'Well, what you may not know is that I come from a family of Holocaust survivors as well.'

I was gobsmacked. My mouth fell open in astonishment.

'My paternal grandfather, Poppa, was French. In early 1944, he and his family were deported to the Drancy Transit Camp and then to Auschwitz. He was lucky enough to be selected for a work detail, but of his family – his parents and two siblings – only he survived.'

'I'm sorry,' was all I could murmur.

Sophie nodded. 'My grandmother was luckier. She was sent from Germany to England in 1939, through the Kindertransport.'

'And her family?'

She simply shook her head.

'My poppa came to Australia in 1948 and met my grandmother, who had emigrated to be with her aunt and uncle, the only family she had left. Poppa studied pharmacy and opened his own chemist shop in Surrey Hills. So, the family was quite well off.'

'Was he…scarred by the experience?' I asked in a hesitant voice.

Sophie shrugged. 'I think he suffered from survivor guilt. He would sit at his desk in his study and stare out the window. Sometimes, if I stayed with them during the holidays, I'd wake to hear him crying.'

'I can relate,' I nodded. 'And what about your maternal grandparents?'

'They were born in Australia and were relatively unscathed.'

'How lucky can you be,' I quipped.

'My parents both grew up in traditional Jewish homes and kept up the traditions. Each Shabbat eve my mother prepared dinner and my father would say the blessings. When we were old enough, Papa insisted we take over. We celebrated the festivals of Passover, Rosh Hashanah, and Yom Kippur. I think it had to do with Jewish continuity. About perpetuating the traditions that would bring a death sentence under the Nazis.'

I smiled and stretched my hand to clasp hers. 'So, it seems we have something else in common besides…you know.'

She blushed and gave my hand a gentle squeeze. We locked eyes, and after a time she said, 'A penny for your thoughts?'

'I was just thinking how beautiful you are,' I murmured.

She lowered her eyes, then looked up at me and said softly, 'Why, thank you.'

I jumped when the waitress appeared, flashing a bright smile.

'What can I get you ladies?'

'Ah, snapper for me please … and sparkling water for two,' Sophie said smoothly, glancing across at me.

'And, uh, I'll have the blue-eye. Can we also have a caprese salad to share?' I asked.

'Excellent choice,' said the waitress, nodding her approval before disappearing towards the kitchen.

Sophie was silent for a long time, then said, 'Thanks for letting me into your world.' She was gently massaging my hand with her thumb. It's a great comfort to know that you understand me.'

I smiled. 'I feel the same way.'

'Good,' said Sophie. 'Now, you were talking about Albert and his obnoxious brother.'

'So…back to the Görings…well, Hermann didn't waste any time after the Anschluss, winding up the local antisemites with speeches about Jewish racial inferiority.'

'Hateful bastard,' muttered Sophie.

I nodded. 'Albert and his sister Olga pleaded with Hermann on behalf of Archduke Josef Ferdinand, the last Habsburg Prince of

Tuscany, who had been imprisoned at the Dachau concentration camp.'

'Really!' Sophie pondered. 'Did it work?'

'Oh yeah,' I replied. 'The next day he was released.'

'I wonder why Hermann agreed,' mused Sophie.

'Funny you should ask,' I said. 'Richard Sonnenfeldt, the translator for the American prosecution team at the Nuremberg trials, wrote in his memoir that Hermann wanted to impress his little brother.'

'Crazy,' remarked Sophie. 'One of history's greatest monsters had a human side, after all.'

'A human side that Albert exploited. He would regularly intercede with his brother for the release of a Jewish friend or a political prisoner. He became a master manipulator of Hermann's ego, calling on his sense of brotherly duty. Albert would say, "Hermann you're so powerful, here's a good Jew who doesn't belong in a concentration camp. Can't you just sign a paper?" And Hermann would respond, "This is the last time I'm going to do this, so don't ask me again." A month later, Albert would be back.'

'What an amazing story,' marvelled Sophie. 'How many did he save?'

'At least a hundred,' I replied. 'He signed passports to help Jews escape the Third Reich, and on one occasion persuaded Reinhard Heydrich to release a group of Czech resistance fighters. Another time, he joined a group of Jewish women in Vienna who had been forced to scrub the cobblestone streets on their knees. When the SS officers inspected his identification, they ordered the scrubbing to stop, realising they could be held responsible for publicly humiliating Göring's brother.'

Neither of us spoke for a time, then the waitress appeared with our food.

'Thank you,' I said as she placed the plates on the table.

'Bon appetit,' smiled Sophie, as she cut into her fish.

'There are many such stories,' I continued. 'Albert once came upon a group of Nazi thugs who had put a sign around an old woman's neck proclaiming, "I'm a Jewish sow". Albert pushed through the mob and punched two Gestapo officers. His life might have ended right there, as the crowd turned on him. But when the SS officers saw his name on his papers, they escorted him to safety.'

'He must have been a man of great courage,' said Sophie.

'And principle,' I added.

'Yes, and principle,' she echoed.

'When Jewish friends in Vienna were arrested,' I continued, 'Albert forged documents to help them escape. And while working at Skoda he collaborated with the Czech underground to sabotage weapons the company was producing. When caught by the Gestapo, he invoked his brother's name to gain his release.'

'There must be whole families who owe their lives to Albert,' said Sophie.

'No doubt about it,' I said, spearing a morsel of fish on my plate. 'He would send trucks to concentration camps with requests for workers. Once loaded, the trucks would drive into a forest and the people would be allowed to escape. He also supplied Jews with exit permits and helped to transport their assets out of Nazi Germany.'

'And the Gestapo had no clue?' Sophie asked.

'Not at first,' I replied. 'But he could only get away with it for so long. By 1944, the Gestapo had issued a warrant that Albert should be killed on sight. He went to ground in Prague and was eventually saved by his brother, who asked Himmler to rescind the warrant.'

'This would make for an amazing book,' said Sophie.

I grinned. 'That's the plan. A doctoral thesis that I can turn into a best seller!'

'So how does the story end?'

'The brothers met for the last time in May 1945 in the exercise courtyard of a jail in Augsburg. Hermann was on his way to Nuremburg for trial and Albert was detained for simply being his brother.'

'Guilt by association,' said Sophie.

I nodded. 'Unjustified in this case. But anyway, Hermann was sentenced to death for war crimes and crimes against humanity. But he cheated the hangman by swallowing a cyanide capsule smuggled into his cell.'

'What a coward!' spat Sophie.

'Oh yeah. One of his most disgusting crimes was the use of concentration camp inmates for medical experiments in the hopes of saving downed German airmen.'

'How?' asked Sophie.

I sighed. 'German pilots were freezing to death in the icy waters of the North Sea. So Hermann Göring ordered the Luftwaffe medical department to try and find ways of restoring their body temperature. So they dumped concentration camp prisoners in tanks of freezing water and experimented with methods to revive them.'

'That's terrible!' muttered Sophie.

'You don't know the half of it,' I replied. 'One of the methods they tried was to place a frozen man between two naked female concentration camp prisoners.'

'That's appalling.'

'And Göring ordered them to conduct pressure-chamber experiments to observe the effects of high altitude on the human body.'

'I...I...I knew Hermann was a murderous degenerate,' stuttered Sophie, 'but I'd never heard of this.' After everything his brother did, it's hard to understand how Albert might have any fondness for him.'

I shrugged. 'Tolstoy divided families into happy and unhappy, but I don't think it's that simple. And perhaps the saddest part of this story is the injustice meted out to Albert merely on account of his name. He was imprisoned at Nuremberg for over a year.'

'Really?'

'Yep. At first, Albert's interrogators didn't believe his story. But many of the people he had saved submitted sworn statements on his behalf. Then a new American interrogator named Victor Parker appeared on the scene. He was a Jewish refugee whose real name was Paschkis. His aunt, Sophie Paschkis, had married the composer Franz Lehár. The Lehárs were among those Albert had helped save. Victor Parker heard from his aunt that Albert had helped Jewish people escape. So Albert's stories were validated and he was released.'

Sophie pushed back in her seat, looked at me and said, 'Thank God for that.'

'The story's not yet over,' I warned. 'Albert was then arrested by the Czechs on charges of Nazi collaboration. However, this time members of the Czech resistance who had worked in the Skoda factory where Albert had been a manager saved him. They testified that Albert helped sabotage Nazi war production and he was again released.'

Sophie smiled and let out a sigh of relief. 'It's like a spy novel.'

'One by Le Carré. They always have sad endings.'

'Why sad?' she asked.

'Well, after the war, Albert was shunned because of his family name. He was unemployable as a Göring, but refused to change his name, which would have been the simple solution. He became an alcoholic, suffered from depression, and after reported infidelities, his third wife, a Czech woman named Mila Klazarova, divorced him. She emigrated with their only child to South America. Albert never saw or spoke to his daughter again. He eked out a modest living as a writer and translator, but mostly lived on his pension with his housekeeper, who was to become his fourth wife.'

'So, the name that once enabled him to save hundreds of Nazi victims became a burden in the end,' Sophie said quietly.

The patter of raindrops on the restaurant window caused me to look across Domain Road at the trees in the park. People passed by beneath umbrellas under a bleak overcast sky. It was as though the world was crying.

'His daughter Elizabeth later said that her mother forced her to write letters, but he never answered them. She interpreted that lack of response as a sign he didn't want her, but who knows?'

Sophie looked solemn. 'Albert's family was another casualty of Nazi madness.'

I shrugged. 'Perhaps, but Elizabeth still respected her father. Apparently, Mila never said a word against him. And Albert was the only German her Czech grandmother respected, or so she said. In his final years, Albert lived on a small government pension and food packages sent by Jews he had saved. He died in obscurity.'

'So sad,' Sophie said.

'Very,' I agreed. 'It seems Albert was a philanderer, but he did the right thing by his last housekeeper. He knew that if he married, his pension would be transferred to his wife on his death. So, he married Brunhilde in 1966, to ensure she would receive his benefits. One week later, he died of pancreatic cancer.'

Sophie shuddered.

'There was no public recognition of his anti-Nazi activities.'

'That's something you can fix,' said Sophie.

'Belatedly,' I replied. 'Albert was the subject of a short write-up in a German magazine when he was still alive. Aside from that, his story remained largely unknown until he became the subject of a TV documentary in 1998. Since then, there have been a couple of biographies, but I think I can do better.'

'How modest,' smiled Sophie.

I laughed and bowed theatrically. 'But seriously, I think I can give Albert the justice he deserves – and the history department agrees.'

'That's great news,' said Sophie, her eyes crinkling in pleasure.

'There's one piece of the puzzle that has yet to be found, and I hope I can help with that.'

'What do you mean?' she asked.

'You're familiar with the Righteous Among the Nations award issued by Yad Vashem in Jerusalem?'

'Of course,' nodded Sophie.

'Well…Yad Vashem has denied that recognition to Albert.'

'That's outrageous!' said Sophie.

'Yeah, despite all the testimonials from Jews he saved from certain death, Yad Vashem said there wasn't enough primary source material to justify the award.'

'That's bureaucratic nonsense!'

I nodded. 'You know, I found an image online of Albert's grave at the Göring family plot in Munich. Apparently, the tombstone was removed because nobody in the family paid the fees. As I looked at it, I envisaged the smoky cabaret dens and bohemian cafés that he would have frequented. I could almost picture him saving that innocent man from the wrath of an antisemitic mob in Vienna. I imagined being a fly on the wall as Albert pleaded with his brother to save innocent Jewish lives. It was a surreal experience.'

'Wow,' was all Sophie could say.

'The Göring family motto was "We are not among those who yield, but among those who believe." In the end, it was only Albert who embodied that principle.'

'So true,' sighed Sophie.

We concentrated on our meals, then Sophie said, 'This has been so interesting. You've taught me a lot. I look forward to reading your thesis.'

'Yeah…about that…'

She looked at me with an expectant smile.

'I'll be spending at least six months digging through the archives in Berlin, Munich and Prague. I hoped…' my voice trailed off.

'Hoped what?' she asked with a smile.

'I hoped you might come with me…at least for part of the time. I have a study grant that will cover accommodation, food and travel. Also, I could help out with your ticket.'

'Wow…that's a surprise,' she said. Her face was wreathed in smiles. 'I think I'd like that.'

'You speak French, right?'

She nodded.

'Then you'll know the term *coup de foudre*.'

Another nod. 'It means lightning strike.'

'As well as love at first sight,' I added. 'When you know, you know.' I took her hand in mine. 'I'm saying that in the short term I want you with me in Europe. And in the long term, I'm saying that…that I hope you'll be my life partner.'

Several moments of silence ensued.

'I'll have to think about it,' she said in a quiet voice.

'You do that, but, in the meantime, can I begin to draw up an itinerary?'

She said nothing, but her smile gave me cause for hope.

Never Forget

'So, let me begin with a question,' said Moishe to the three dozen VCE students from Ben Yehuda College sitting opposite. 'Have any of you heard the name Emanuel Ringelblum?'

They were seated around a large table in the Melbourne Holocaust Museum, with sunlight streaming through floor-to-ceiling glass doors, burnishing the glossy hair of the teenagers.

Moishe glanced around the room, noting the blank faces opposite.

'No worries,' he smiled. 'How about the Warsaw Ghetto? I'm sure you've all heard of that.'

A young girl with red hair raised a hand.

'And what's your name?' asked Moishe.

'Rachel,' replied the girl quietly.

'Please go on,' Moishe nodded.

'It's a neighbourhood in Warsaw where the Germans imprisoned the Jews before sending them to concentration camps.'

'Very good, Rachel,' smiled Moishe. 'The Warsaw Ghetto was a walled-off section of the city around 3.5 square kilometres in area that was created by the Germans in November 1940. Now, your school is in Caulfield South. Does anyone know its geographic size?'

After several seconds of silence, Moishe spoke again. 'Before you came, I did a bit of research. Caulfield South takes up an area of 3.3 square kilometres, which is almost the same size as the Warsaw Ghetto. Do any of you know what the population of Caulfield South is?'

'Ten thousand?' shrugged a blond boy with a mouthful of shiny braces.

'According to the last census, 12,300 people. Now, does anyone want to estimate how many Jews were forced into the ghetto?'

Silence.

'No one?' pressed Moishe as he glanced from face to face. 'Well, the answer is over 450,000.'

Gasps of astonishment erupted from young people around the table.

'That's right,' nodded Moishe. 'So let's do the maths. Over thirty-five times the population of Caufield crammed into a space that's just slightly smaller. That means two or even three families were forced to live in a single room. Diseases like typhus were rampant. And when you add starvation rations to that systematic overcrowding, the result was scurvy and rickets and a public health disaster. Which, of course, is precisely what the Nazis intended.'

'You mean the Germans wanted to starve them to death?' asked a slender boy wearing a *kippah* on his head.

'Exactly,' said Moishe. 'And with considerable success. Almost 100,000 Jews died of malnutrition and associated diseases.'

'What happened to the other 350,000?' asked Rachel.

'Didn't you study this in your Holocaust curriculum at Ben Yehuda?' asked Moishe.

'We learned about Auschwitz and some of our class went on March of the Living,' replied the boy with braces. 'But I don't remember us studying that much about the Warsaw Ghetto.'

'Well, let's do what we can to fill in the gaps,' sighed Moishe. 'So it turned out that death by famine wasn't efficient enough for the Nazis. They rounded up most of the ghetto residents and put them on trains to the Treblinka death camp where they were gassed and their bodies were incinerated.'

The students sat motionless in stunned silence until Moishe spoke.

'It's a horrific story, but it's that story that brings us to my original question…who was Emanuel Ringelblum? Ringelblum is the primary reason we know what we know about the Warsaw Ghetto. The archive of material he collected and preserved gives unique and irreplaceable insights into daily life for the half a million Jews confined there.'

'Did he die?' asked Rachel. 'Did the Germans kill him?'

'We'll get to that,' sighed Moishe, 'but for now let's focus on his activities in the ghetto. Fair enough?'

The students nodded.

'Good. Ringelblum was a trained historian with a doctorate from Warsaw University. So he decided to do what he knew best: to document the horrors that the Nazis were inflicting on the ghetto. He assembled a team of people, including an Orthodox rabbi and Jewish writers and editors. They called themselves by the codename *Oneg Shabbat*, which means Sabbath Joy. My grandfather was a member of that group.'

'Wow, that's amazing,' marvelled the boy with braces.

'And what's your name?' asked Moishe.

'Daniel,' the boy replied with a cheery smile.

'Well, Daniel, do you know the word *zayde* in Yiddish?'

'Sorry,' Daniel shrugged, his face reddening with embarrassment. 'My family isn't that…observant.'

'Don't worry about it,' said Moishe in a tone of reassurance. *Zayde* is the Yiddish word for grandfather, and my *zayde* told me that the group would meet behind closed doors each Saturday afternoon.'

'Why behind closed doors?' asked the boy wearing the *kippah*.

'You'll have to tell me your name,' smiled Moishe.

'Ben,' the boy replied. 'Sorry.'

'Nice to meet you, Ben,' said Moishe. 'They met behind closed doors because the Germans were running a sophisticated disinformation campaign. They built a model concentration camp at Terezin in Czechoslovakia where a handful of prominent Jewish prisoners were held in very good conditions. This is where the Nazis would put these special prisoners on display to the Red Cross, foreign diplomats and international press to disprove stories of atrocities against the Jews. So what do you think would happen if the Germans discovered that their abuses in the Warsaw Ghetto were documented by the *Oneg Shabbat* group?'

'Everyone in the group would have been killed,' said Ben.

'Precisely,' Moishe affirmed. 'So, during the day they took notes on life in the ghetto, the cruelty and maliciousness of the Germans, the hunger of the Jews, the living conditions, their medical and sanitary conditions, their schools and underground publications, the rumours, their jokes and even their street life. Then, at night, they would meet in secret to incorporate those notes into comprehensive reports.'

'What sort of information did they collect?' asked Rachel.

Moishe shrugged. 'They described daily life in the ghetto… and daily death. They wrote about the bakers' trucks that would circulate each morning to collect the bodies of Jews who had died overnight from malnutrition and disease. They described the mice and rats gnawing at the carcasses that lay in the street waiting to be collected. And starving people scavenging through rubbish bins and gutters looking for food and cigarette butts to trade.'

'Why didn't people escape?' asked Daniel.

'Some did,' replied Moishe. 'But it wasn't that simple or easy. The entire area was walled off and guarded by armed sentries. The Jews within were forced into a desperate struggle for survival against disease, starvation and random Nazi brutality. The daily food ration provided one-tenth of the required minimum daily calorie intake for a healthy adult. So, many of those who got out of the ghetto returned with supplies of food they smuggled in to help their families.'

'What did people do all day inside the ghetto?' asked a burly boy with wrestler's shoulders.

'And your name is…?' asked Moishe.

'Simon,' replied the wrestler.

'Well, Simon, they went about living their lives as best they could,' sighed Moishe. 'Despite everything, you had artists and intellectuals who continued their creative endeavours. There were underground libraries, youth movements, schools and even a symphony orchestra. Books, study, music and theatre served as an escape from the harsh reality of daily life.'

'You said earlier that Jews were transported to the death camp at Treblinka. When did that start?' Ben asked.

'In July 1942,' Moishe replied. 'When the first deportation orders came in from the Germans, Adam Czerniaków, the chairman of the Ghetto Jewish Council…the *Judenrat*…refused to prepare lists of persons for deportation. Rather than comply with that German demand, he took his own life on the 23rd of July 1942.'

Moishe noticed that Rachel's eyes glistened with tears as she wiped her cheek with the back of her hand.

'What sort of documentary evidence did Ringelblum collect?' asked Simon.

'Diaries, reports, posters and Nazi decrees. Over 25,000 pages of documentation that described daily life, the activities of the *Judenrat* and social relief organisations. They also recorded the deportations from July to September 1942, and reports of Jews being gassed at the death camps at Chelmno and Treblinka.'

'What did they do with those documents?' asked Ben.

'They were transmitted to the Polish Home Army, which smuggled the information to the Polish Government-in-Exile in London. In December 1942, Polish Foreign-Minister-in-Exile Count Edward Raczynski made a formal statement denouncing the murder of Jews and promising punishment for the guilty.'

Rachel's hand rose slowly…tentatively.

'Yes?' nodded Moishe.

'I read somewhere a while ago that new documents were uncovered at the Vatican showing that the Pope knew what was happening to the Jews,' she said, half in question and half in statement.

Moishe's mouth curled in a diplomatic smile worthy of the most polished DFAT ambassador. 'Let's just say that the behaviour of

Pope Pius XII during World War II is the topic of vigorous debate among scholars. But I suggest we leave that controversy to the historians. Instead, I'd like to talk about the role played by Emanuel Ringelblum in the Warsaw Ghetto Uprising.'

'Last year I saw a movie on TV about that,' said Simon.

'Which one?' asked Moishe. 'There have been several.'

'The one about a piano player.'

'Entitled *The Pianist*,' grinned Moishe, triggering a wave of laughter that swept through the student audience. 'But yes, in April 1943, the two Jewish armed underground organisations joined forces to strike against the Germans. Ringelblum not only participated in the rebellion, but he recorded the events leading up to it.'

'Why were there two underground groups?' asked Rachel.

'Because the Jewish community tends to be very political,' Moishe said. 'It's not for nothing that we say "two Jews, three opinions".'

Another wave of laughter came from the students.

'And so, there were two rival underground militias in the ghetto, the socialist Jewish Combat Organisation, or ŻOB, and the conservative Jewish Military Union, or ŻZW. But in early 1943, they came together to form a united front to fight against the Germans.'

'Why so late?' asked Ben. 'If the ghetto was created in November 1940 and the deportations began in 1942, why did they wait until 1943 to fight back?'

'A great question,' nodded Moishe. 'Try and think about it this way. When the first reports of gassings at Treblinka trickled back to the ghetto, a lot of people simply didn't believe it. They didn't believe that a modern, civilised country like Germany would instigate a program of mass murder. Especially when it was fighting a two-front war against superior enemies.'

'America, Russia and Britain,' said Simon.

'And Australia,' Rachel added.

'And Australia,' echoed Moishe. 'Our diggers were fighting against the Afrika Korps in Libya and Egypt. So, when the evidence of mass murder became impossible to ignore, the Jewish underground groups faced the challenge of acquiring weapons. They were able to buy some guns and ammunition on the black market and the Polish Home Army provided a few more. But all that took time.'

Ben nodded his understanding.

'Then in January 1943, the Germans stepped up the frequency of deportations to Treblinka. Their objective was to eradicate the ghetto by sending all remaining Jews to the gas chambers. So the ŻOB and ŻZW felt they couldn't delay any longer.'

'What did they do?' asked Rachel.

'On the 18th of January, a group of resistance fighters joined a crowd of Jews at the *Umschlagplätze*, the holding area where trains to Treblinka were loaded with people destined for death. On a prearranged signal, the Jewish fighters pulled out their hidden pistols and opened fire. They managed to kill around a dozen Germans and wound several dozen more while suffering many casualties of their own. But their most important achievement was bringing deportations to a temporary halt.'

'Amazing,' Daniel marvelled.

'Yes, it was,' agreed Moishe. 'The battle of the 18th of January galvanised the spirit of resistance throughout the ghetto. People began to defy deportation orders and go to ground in hiding places. The ŻOB and ŻZW constructed bunkers and fortified positions that overlooked access points to the ghetto.'

'Who were the leaders of those underground groups?' asked Rachel.

The ŻOB's was led by twenty-four-year-old Mordechai Anielewicz. He began as a member of the conservative Beitar

Zionist youth movement. But he later changed his views and joined the socialist *Shomer Hatza'ir*. The leader of the conservative ŻZW was a former Polish army officer named Paweł Frenkiel. The uprising began on the evening Passover Seder.'

'Was that intentional?' asked Daniel, his face darkening with a frown.

'Yeah, were they adding insult to injury?' echoed Simon.

'We can't know for sure,' shrugged Moishe. 'But I wouldn't be surprised if they thought it was a great joke to launch the final assault against the ghetto on the Jewish holiday of liberation. But if so, it was a joke that blew up in their faces…literally.'

There was some nervous laughter, but as Moishe glanced around the room he was gratified by the looks of rapt fascination on the faces of his audience.

'The German column was hit by homemade grenades, Molotov cocktails and gunfire, mostly from pistols and a couple of submachine guns. The shocked SS troops beat a retreat beyond the ghetto walls, leaving a dozen men dead on the street behind them.'

'That's good,' growled Simon.

'Because of this failure, the original SS commander was replaced by *Standartenführer* Jürgen Stroop, the SS and Police Leader in Warsaw. Stroop was experienced in anti-partisan warfare and brought two thousand troops, reinforced with artillery and tanks, to the task of wiping out the ghetto.'

'And what about casualties in the Jewish Resistance?' asked Daniel, concerned.

'The ŻOB and ŻZW agreed to put aside their ideological differences and fight as a combined force. There were about seven hundred Jewish fighters in all who were armed with pistols, homemade grenades, a few automatic weapons and rifles. They had no military training, but made up for it with fierce determination to fight for their dignity. They had no illusions about survival.'

'Wow,' muttered Ben.

'The Jews did have the advantage of knowing the local terrain. They waged a guerrilla war of hit and run, ambushing the Germans and then retreating to bunkers across rooftops and through underground tunnels. The remaining Jews of the ghetto thwarted German roundups, hiding rather than following orders to assemble at the *Umschlagplätze*.'

'How long did they hold out?' asked Rachel, her face solemn.

'For twenty-six days. In the end, the Germans went block by block with flamethrowers and explosives. By the 8th of May 1943, the Germans finally succeeded in razing the ghetto to the ground. Anielewicz and many of his staff commanders are thought to have committed suicide to avoid capture. On the 16th of May, Stroop reported to Berlin that the former Jewish Quarter in Warsaw was no more.'

'Were there any survivors?' asked Daniel, his eyes awash with tears.

'About 7,000 Jews were killed during the fighting,' sighed Moishe. 'Of those who survived, 42,000 were sent to forced labour camps and the Majdanek death camp, and another 7,000 were gassed at Treblinka. A handful of fighters managed to escape through the Warsaw sewer system.'

Moishe paused and flashed an uncharacteristically shy smile. 'It just so happens that my grandfather was one of those fighters who survived.'

Gasps of astonishment burst from the students.

'If the entire ghetto was blown up by the Germans, what happened to Ringelblum's records?' asked Simon.

'Now that's a really interesting part of the story,' replied Moishe. 'The *Oneg Shabbat* group buried the documents in caches before the outbreak of the rebellion. Ten clay-covered tin boxes were discovered in September 1946. Although they were damaged by water, their contents were still salvageable. And in December 1950, two metal milk cans were found in a cellar of a ruined house in what had been the ghetto. The material within was in much better shape and included issues of underground newspapers, public notices by the *Judenrat*, concert invitations, milk coupons, chocolate wrappers and reports on deportation actions. Today, this archive serves as a major source for the history of the Warsaw Ghetto.'

'Did they find all of it?' asked Ben.

Moishe shook his head. 'No. There were stories of a third milk can. But despite extensive searches, it was never found. Some people say it's now located beneath the Chinese Embassy building.'

'So I guess we'll never know where it is,' said Daniel.

'Tell us more about Ringelblum,' pressed Rachel.

'Okay,' nodded Moishe. 'He joined the Jewish self-help society, ZTOS, after Germany invaded Poland in September 1939. ZTOS set up soup kitchens that offered not only food, but also provided opportunities for people to socialise. In addition, it served as a cover for underground political activities. Ringelblum arranged employment for the thousands of Jewish teachers, writers and intellectuals in the ghetto who were left with no means of support.'

'What about before the war?' Ben asked.

Moishe coughed and poured himself a glass of water from a jug on the table, taking a long swallow to settle his throat. 'Emanuel Ringelblum was born in the town of Galician Buchach in 1900. At the time, Galicia was part of the Austro-Hungarian Empire. When he was a teenager, his family moved to the city of Nowy Sącz in what is now Poland. A few years later the Ringelblums moved again, this time to Warsaw. In 1922 he enrolled in the Faculty of Philosophy at Warsaw University, completing his PhD five years later. His academic focus was on the history of Polish Jewry from the late Middle Ages until the Napoleonic emancipation. Along the way, he married Yehudit Herman and they had one child, a boy they named Uri.'

'Did he become a professor?' asked Simon.

'No, he taught history at the Yehudiya High School for girls in Warsaw. He was active in Jewish politics, joining *Poalei Zion*, a Marxist–Zionist group.'

'That sounds weird,' said Daniel. 'I read somewhere that Marxists believe in internationalism. But isn't Zionism a form of Jewish nationalism? So how could they be both?'

'That's an excellent question,' said Moishe, 'They believed in the creation of a socialist regime in Palestine where Jews could escape antisemitism. But some members couldn't accept that and broke away to create a rival group. Remember what I said about two Jews and three opinions? Well, that's a good example.'

Moishe paused to allow the students' laughter to subside.

'In 1923, Ringelblum helped to create the Young Historians Circle, a group that advocated for Jewish civil rights in Poland. He found work at the Institute for Jewish Research and published over 100 articles in academic journals. He also joined the *Landkentenish* movement, which promoted the virtues of life in the countryside.'

'He was a very busy man,' observed Rachel.

'A veritable dynamo,' laughed Moishe. 'In addition to all that, he also worked for the American Jewish Joint Distribution Committee, an international social service agency. He was central to the establishment of Jewish free loan societies. Does anyone know what a free loan society is?'

There was silence in the library for several moments until Simon raised his hand.

'Yes Simon?'

'Ah…a society that provides loans for free?' he grinned impishly, triggering a spate of laughter from his fellow students.

'Not exactly,' grinned Moishe. 'In fact, they were a serious solution to a serious problem. Antisemitism was deeply engrained in Polish society in those days. So much so, that it was impossible for Jewish individuals and businesses to obtain credit from Polish banks. So these Jewish free loan societies…there were almost 900 of them…would offer 50 per cent of the amount needed for the loan. For example, let's say you were a Jewish businessman who wanted to found a company of some sort. A free loan society would lend you half on reasonable repayment terms, while you would have to come up with the other 50 per cent on your own. That's how it worked.'

'That's amazing,' marvelled Rachel.

'Wait, there's more,' grinned Moishe. 'In October 1938, Emanuel Ringelblum was appointed to lead the Joint Distribution Committee relief team in Zbąszyń, a small town on the German–Polish border.'

'What happened there?' Ben asked.

'At that time the Nazi regime expelled six thousand Polish Jews who had been living in Germany. Even though these Jews held Polish citizenship, the government in Warsaw didn't want to accept them.'

Rachel shook her head. 'That's terrible.'

Moishe nodded. 'Yes. You had around 17,000 people…men women and children…trapped in limbo along the Polish–German border. So Emanuel Ringelblum organised food supplies, a hospital and health services, a social welfare system and even a court of arbitration. He was a truly amazing man.'

'What happened to him?' asked Simon. 'Did he survive the war?'

Moishe shook his head. 'Alas, no. Just before the uprising, in March 1943, Ringelblum and his family were smuggled out of the ghetto into the non-Jewish part of Warsaw. But he chose to return just before the fighting began. He was captured and taken to a German labour camp, but the Polish underground helped him to escape. He returned to Warsaw and joined his family in hiding, but he was betrayed to the Germans by a local Pole and arrested.'

A sad silence settled over the library until Moishe broke it. 'The Polish underground found the betrayer and killed him.'

'Good,' snorted Simon.

Moishe nodded. 'Emanuel was confined to a cell with his son Uri while his wife was locked up in the women's section. A plot was hatched to move him from the death cells to a section from where prisoners were sent to work in Germany. But Ringelblum refused.'

'Why?' moaned Rachel. 'Why would he reject the chance to stay alive?'

'Well, according to the man who snuck into his cell to propose the plan of escape, Ringelblum asked about his son and wife. The answer was obvious…he would have to leave them behind. And Emanuel Ringelblum was not prepared to do that. "I prefer to do *Kiddush Ha-Shem* with my family," he's reported to have said. It's the Hebrew for the sanctification of God's name.' He paused and looked around at their young faces. 'Emanuel Ringelblum, his wife and son were shot by a German firing squad in March 1944.'

'He was a hero,' murmured Daniel, his eyes glistening with tears.

'Indeed, he was,' agreed Moishe. 'And as a mark of respect, the Jewish Historical Institute in Warsaw bears his name.'

Moishe glanced around the room at the flushed faces and reddened eyes of his audience. 'Are there any additional questions?'

After several moments of silence, he nodded. 'Then all that remains is for me to thank you for your attendance and attention today.'

Wannsee Conference – Protocol

'I saw a disturbing documentary on the TV yesterday,' Otto announced midway through dinner. 'About the Wannsee Conference. Have you heard of it?'

'Enough to know we both would have been on Hitler's hit list,' grinned Henry, his husband of five years and life partner for far longer.

'That's right. It wasn't only the Jews that Hitler wanted to exterminate. He also targeted gays, Romani, Slavs, the mentally ill…'

Henry gazed across the table, noting for the umpteenth time the physical attributes that he still found attractive after a lifetime together – Otto's tall, slender physique, blue eyes and perfect oval face.

Otto was a doctor who had dedicated his life to geriatric medicine. Gentle, compassionate, he was a man well suited to his profession. Henry's heart still lifted when Otto took his hand, or smiled at him with such kindness. He found Otto's tenderness both endearing and sustaining.

Henry was less fond of the image that confronted him each morning in the mirror, although he would never admit it…even to Otto. His upright bearing was meant to compensate for his lack of height, and to constrain his stout midriff, but Henry feared it did neither. Yet he was an extrovert, a barrister who dominated the courtroom with confidence and flair. His emotional intelligence enabled him to read people, a talent that came in handy when he cross-examined witnesses, who he often reduced to tears. One of his colleagues at the bar once commented that Henry's performance in front of juries should be worthy of a legal Oscar if there were such a thing. Having learned discipline through military drill during his short time in school cadets, he was a determined man who knew how to get what he wanted.

Otto and Henry first met on the beach at Portofino. Henry had just graduated from Melbourne Law while Otto had finished his internship year at Charité Hospital in Berlin. The attraction was instantaneous. After a long-distance relationship of several years, while Otto qualified as a specialist in geriatric medicine, he emigrated to Australia.

They agreed that Otto would convert to Henry's faith of Progressive Judaism. That meant he would turn his back on Christianity, the church, its Friday fish fries, the bacon for breakfast and the wine with wafers on Sundays. They agreed their intended children should be brought up in a Jewish home.

They were lucky enough to be in the House of Representatives public gallery when the bill legalising gay marriage was passed on the 7th of December 2017. The next month, Henry and Otto took their own vows in front of Rabbi Gersh Lazarow at Temple Beth Israel in East St Kilda. Henry smiled at the memory.

'It's no laughing matter!' Otto barked across the dinner table. 'I hate the Nazis! I hate them! Hate them!'

Henry looked at his husband in shock before murmuring, 'So do I, Otto. So do I.'

'They filmed the documentary at the same time of the year,' Otto continued. 'It was a snowy morning on the 20th of January 1942.'

'Aha,' Henry replied, unsure where this was going.

'Fifteen men, eight of whom had doctorates, attended an invitation-only conference,' Otto said, 'at an elegant, opulent villa…'

'At Wannsee,' Henry concluded. 'Remember, we went there. Golf courses, the lake, leafy avenues…I've seen photos of the building, but I don't think we visited it.'

'Wannsee House is a Holocaust memorial and museum now. Apparently Joseph Wulf, a historian and Holocaust survivor, proposed during the 1960s to turn Wannsee House into a Holocaust Museum, but the West German government couldn't be bothered. Wulf later killed himself, but his idea ultimately triumphed. On the fiftieth anniversary of the conference, on the 20th of January 1992, his idea was realised.'

'I'm sorry we didn't visit it,' said Henry.

'Apparently, in preparation for the conference, Adolph Eichmann calculated the number of Jews throughout Europe.' Otto ploughed on. 'In all, eleven million Jews were to be slated for death. Half were in countries under the direct control of the Reich, and the other half were in countries at war with Germany.'

'At least Eichmann got what he deserved when the Israelis caught up with him in Argentina,' said Henry.

'Yeah, twenty years later,' groused Otto. 'But in 1942 he was cracking jokes while planning mass murder. They sat around a big oak table while white-jacketed waiters plied them with brandy and cigars.'

'Evil bastards,' muttered Henry.

Otto nodded. 'And the meeting was presided over by Reinhard Heydrich, the head of the *Reichssicherheitshauptamt*, a mouthful that translates as Reich Security Main Office.'

'Heydrich got his as well later that year, didn't he?' asked Henry. 'I saw a film about it. *Anthropoid,* I think it was…But why are you so interested in the Wannsee Conference?'

Otto forged on, oblivious to Henry's question. 'Heydrich opened with an account of the anti-Jewish measures taken in Germany since the Nazis' seizure of power in 1933. He announced that between 1933 and October 1941, 537,000 Jews had emigrated from Germany, Austria and Czechoslovakia. But that wasn't enough. And Himmler had prohibited further Jewish emigration anyway.'

Henry looked at Otto in silence, feeling a niggling sense of disquiet over his husband's unusual behaviour.

'Heydrich announced that Jews would now be deported to the East for forced labour, but that wasn't enough.'

'Merely a step towards the final solution of the Jewish question,' Henry observed.

'No doubt about that. Remember that the Babi Yar massacre took place in September 1941 – 33,000 killed over three days at the ravine outside Kiev. And by January 1942, SS *Einsatzgruppen* had been shooting Jews throughout Russia for six months already.'

'I remember reading the Yevtushenko poem at uni,' Henry said, blinking as he recited the words of *Babi Yar*. "Today I am as old in years as all the Jewish people."

'So it's clear the orders came from the top,' said Otto, hesitating long enough to acknowledge Henry's poetic recitation.

'Yes, Hitler must have approved of what was going on. The problem was the shooting operations were slow and traumatic for the *Einsatzgruppen* troops.'

'Poor dears,' said Henry with bitter sarcasm. 'Hope they all hanged themselves.'

'Indeed,' agreed Otto, 'but the fact remains there were simply too many Jews to shoot. The Nazis felt that they had to mechanise mass murder in order to achieve their goal of a Jew-free Europe. In December 1941, Hitler announced to the senior Nazi leadership a policy of total annihilation. After Himmler met with Hitler, he noted in his appointment book: "Jewish question – to be exterminated as partisans."'

'But Otto, we both know this. Why upset yourself?' Henry said quietly.

Otto continued as if Henry hadn't spoken. 'It was all contained in the briefing paper Eichmann prepared for Heydrich before the Wannsee meeting. It called for able-bodied Jews to be separated by gender and transported to the East where they would work on roads and railway lines. The expectation was that most of these people would die from overwork and poor treatment. But the remainder...the elderly and children...were marked for death immediately. The only question was how.'

Henry filled his wine glass and took a long swig before muttering, 'Evil beyond belief.'

'Yes,' said Otto. 'The children had to be killed in order to cut off the "seed of a Jewish revival", as they put it.'

Henry examined his wine.

'Hope I'm not boring you.' Otto fixed his gaze on Henry.

'Not at all. What makes you ask?'

'Just wondering. You seem distracted.'

'Of course I'm interested. It's just…that this is all so terrible.'

'But important,' said Otto. 'So, at Wannsee, Heydrich conveyed Hitler's instructions to prepare a "total solution of the Jewish question". It took only ninety minutes for the participants, who included bureaucrats from the transport and justice ministries, to endorse a plan to murder every Jew in Europe.'

'Is something bothering you, other than the current discussion about Nazis?' asked Henry.

Otto shrugged.

Henry had sensed something strange about Otto's demeanour. Now he thought about it, there had always been something reserved about Otto, throughout their entire relationship and more so during their marriage. He hadn't wanted to admit it, but it often made him feel uneasy. He'd tried to ignore it, but it had always been there, just under the surface.

Meanwhile, Otto was continuing with his disquisition, heedless of Henry's knitted brow and solemn face.

'The participants at the Wannsee Conference were informed of extermination methods that had already been tried and found wanting. The gas vans at Chelmno proved less than efficient at the sort of mass murder Heydrich was envisioning.'

'Otto, this is all too depressing. Can we change the subject, perhaps?' Henry pleaded. 'You've made me lose my appetite.'

'No we can't!' Otto bellowed as Henry shrank back in his chair in shock. 'And I'm appalled that you're thinking about food when we're discussing this!'

'You mean you're discussing it,' said Henry. 'I just wanted to eat dinner.'

'The Nazis were also murdering the Polish and Russian intelligentsia,' Otto said. 'Shortly after the invasion of the Soviet Union, the German army circulated the *Kommissarbefehl*, or commissar order, which called for the summary execution of all captured communist party members.'

'I know, I know all this, Otto,' Henry said quietly, but Otto persisted. 'Heydrich focused the discussion at Wannsee on the status of people who were half or quarter Jews under the Nuremberg Laws of 1935, and Jews married to non-Jews. After all, they'd had to define who was a Jew for the purposes of deportation.'

'The banal bureaucracy of mass murder,' muttered Henry.

'Quite,' agreed Otto. 'To widen the circle of victims, Heydrich ordered a rewrite of the laws so that people with two Jewish grandparents would be treated as Jews, and people with one Jewish grandparent would be treated as German. If a person was not Jewish, but was married to a Jew or lived in, or identified with, the Jewish community, he or she would be regarded as a Jew and condemned.'

'Presumably, that meant the slaughter of many people who never thought of themselves as Jewish,' said Henry.

'Quite true,' Otto nodded. 'They used euphemisms to conceal what they were doing. Rather than words like shooting or gassing, they spoke of "*sonderbehandlung*", which translates as "special handling" but in reality meant murder.'

'Vile assholes,' was all Henry could say.

'Heydrich addressed the conference for nearly an hour, apparently, followed by thirty minutes of questions and comments. Economics bureaucrat Erich Neumann argued for the exemption of Jews who were working in industries vital to the war effort and for whom no replacements were available. Heydrich assured him that this was already the policy; such Jews would not be killed.'

'They'd only be worked to death like beasts,' said Henry.

Otto lowered his head in agreement. 'Göring also wanted to save skilled Jewish workers. But SS *Reichsführer* Heinrich Himmler insisted that all Jews must be killed. And at Wannsee, Reinhard Heydrich insisted that Himmler's policy be put into action. A senior official from the office of the Governor-General for Occupied Poland, Josef Bühler, expressed hope that the killings would commence as soon as possible. He informed the attendees that the 2.5 million Jews in Poland could be murdered on the spot if they were declared unfit for work.'

'I've heard enough,' wailed Henry. 'Please let's talk about something else.'

'As the conference proceeded and the cognac flowed, the conversation around the table became more direct,' Otto continued like a man possessed, ignoring Henry's obvious distress.

'Euphemisms were discarded and the men began to compare different methods of murder using clear language. But as the confab wound down, Heydrich told Eichmann to make sure the minutes of the meeting did not include verbatim quotes. And before dissemination, the minutes were edited by Heydrich himself. But all in all, Heydrich was pleased with the meeting. He thought he might meet with resistance from some of the bureaucrats who attended. But from the Foreign Ministry to the Ministry of Justice, they all came on board.'

Henry's brow creased in a baffled frown. 'But, if the meeting minutes were written in opaque euphemism, how do we know all this?'

'Because the euphemisms weren't so opaque,' Otto explained. 'Most copies of the minutes were destroyed at the end of the war as participants sought to escape prosecution for war crimes. But in 1947, a copy was found by a US prosecutor at Nuremberg in the files of the German Foreign Office.'

'Lucky the Germans are such fastidious record-keepers,' said Henry.

'True,' said Otto, 'but think of it this way. Heydrich didn't call the meeting to make new decisions on the Jewish question because mass killings of Jews were already underway. The extermination camp was under construction at Belzec at the time of the conference.'

'So why was the conference convened?' asked Henry.

'To determine the scope of deportations and ensure the fate of the deportees became an SS matter. Heydrich was determined to ensure the cooperation of the various departments by imposing his own authority on the various ministries and agencies involved in Jewish policy matters.'

'So what you're saying is that these bastards may have been mad as rabid dogs, but they weren't stupid,' said Henry.

'Not quite,' replied Otto. 'Heydrich was a mad dog, whose death couldn't come soon enough, but there were countless underlings who were prepared to accept his dictates. What the Wannsee Conference demonstrates so brutally is how far antisemitism had infiltrated the bloodstream of that most educated and sophisticated society – the same culture that produced Bach and Goethe also produced Himmler and Heydrich.'

'I still find it hard to imagine how such a horror could have happened,' Henry mumbled.

'Step by step,' replied Otto. 'It began once the Nazis came to power in 1933. They launched a massive propaganda campaign to convince Germans that Jews were racially inferior and verminous polluters of Aryan blood who had to be eradicated. In September 1935, the Nuremberg Laws stripped Jews of their German citizenship and prohibited marriages or intimate relations between Jews and non-Jews of Germanic extraction. Jewish property was confiscated and Jews were excluded from the professions and from universities...'

'Yes, yes, I know, of course I know all this, Otto.'

Otto rose from his seat and began pacing back and forth.

Henry's hands were trembling. He squeezed his fingers together. 'Otto, there's something going on here and you need to tell me what it is.'

Otto cast a sidelong glance at him. 'What do you mean?'

'Something's not right. I know you better than anybody. So what's going on?' pressed Henry.

A long silence ensued and Henry could hear the patter of raindrops hitting the glass.

At last Otto spoke. 'It wasn't long before we were married,' he said, breathing hard as he wiped a welling tear from the corner of his eye. 'I finally worked up the courage to do some research on an ancestry website.'

Moments passed, but Henry let the silence be. 'I discovered that what I feared was true,' Otto said.

'What do you mean just after we were married?' Henry asked. 'That was five years ago! So what's this terrible secret you've been hiding from me all this time?'

Otto's chin trembled. 'My maternal grandfather was a member of the Hitler Youth and then a member of the SS.'

'Naw!' exclaimed Henry, shaking his head. 'There must be some mistake.'

'No mistake,' muttered Otto. 'I went through the process three times.'

'I'm so sorry, Otto. I know how proud I am of my grandfather fighting in North Africa with the 9th Australian Division; I can only imagine the pain of knowing your grandfather was in the SS. What kind of SS man was he? Was he in the Waffen SS?'

'Oh, no,' said Otto. 'My grandfather got nowhere near the front lines. With a PhD from the University of Munich, he was much too valuable to serve as cannon fodder. As a matter of fact, I suspect he may have attended the conference at Wannsee.'

'Well, that explains your obsessiveness,' Henry said. 'But it doesn't explain why you've been keeping it from me all this time.'

'Growing up, I knew my grandfather served in the war, because my mother told me,' said Otto, his voice now barely audible. 'He was a cold and unloving man who was very suspicious of strangers.'

'Maybe he was afraid of ending up like Eichmann,' Henry snorted.

'The Nazis were bastards. I'm not ashamed of being German, but I am ashamed of what my grandfather did and what my country did.'

Henry shook his head. 'I don't believe in intergenerational guilt so I don't blame you for what your grandfather may have done before you were born. But I don't understand why you never saw fit to tell me.'

Otto shrugged. 'I guess I was ashamed.'

'It's a question of trust,' replied Henry. 'The fact that you kept this family secret from me is distressing. I can't help wondering what else you might be hiding.'

'But—'

'Right now, there's nothing you can say that will make this better.' Henry gathered his plate and empty glass and left the table without looking back. He called over his shoulder to Otto, 'I'm sleeping in the guest room tonight. Right now, all I know is that trust is like a piece of glass. Once it's shattered it's damn near impossible to restore.'

To Kill the Führer

'*Vater*, how did *Opa* die?' asked Catherine. 'I know the story about a seizure, but I need to know the truth.'

She was seated in front of the heavy oak desk that occupied the centre of my office at Stuttgart Town Hall.

Seeking a moment to collect my thoughts, I glanced at the *Oberbürgermeister's* robe hanging from a wooden coat rack beside the door before returning my gaze to my daughter.

'It was suicide,' I murmured, 'but not really. Hitler gave your *opa* a choice between a public show trial and taking his own life.

Standing trial would have meant he'd lose everything. The house…
his pension…maybe even prison for *Oma* and us. So, he chose to
swallow poison.'

After a moment's silence, Catherine nodded. 'That's what I
wanted to know,' she said. 'Thanks.'

As we sat silently, I saw her shoulders relax a little.

'Why was he forced to commit suicide?' she asked. 'After all, he
was the Desert Fox! Wasn't he one of Germany's greatest generals?'

'Hitler believed that your *opa* was involved in the plot to
assassinate him, the last one, on the 20th of July 1944. The Nazis
knew it would cause a major scandal if *Opa* was publicly branded a
traitor, so they offered him the option of suicide or trial. The Nazis
then ascribed his death to complications from a war wound.'

A sceptical frown darkened Catherine's face. 'But wouldn't a
public trial have been better? After all, he would have been able to
defend himself.'

I snorted. 'It would have been a complete farce. The court
would not have upheld our standards of law, Catherine. The judge
would probably have been Ronald Friesler, the same thug in judicial
robes who sent Sophie Scholl to the guillotine. As I said before, he
wanted to spare me, your aunt Gertrude and your grandmother.

So, he swallowed cyanide…on the 14th of October 1944…and
was buried with full military honours.'

'Was *Opa* really involved in the plot to kill Hitler?'

'I don't know; opinions differ,' I said. 'Another German general
said that *Opa* believed the entire Nazi leadership needed to be killed
if the war were to be ended.'

'I know the plot failed,' Catherine said. 'But what happened to
the conspirators?'

'The bomb only ended up wounding Hitler. It was planted in the
Führerbunker by Lieutenant Colonel Claus von Stauffenberg. Over
the following months, the Gestapo conducted a massive roundup

that relied on information acquired through torture. Stauffenberg was one of the lucky ones. He was executed by firing squad while many of the others were hanged from meat hooks with nooses made of piano wire. By the end, almost five thousand people were killed. It was a bloodbath.'

'I've heard it said that the July 1944 plotters were opportunists,' said Catherine. 'That they only moved against Hitler after it was obvious Germany was losing the war.'

'Not true,' I said with a shake of my head. 'There was a coup planned as early as 1938, but Hitler was too heavily guarded. The conspirators couldn't get near him. There were other plots too. A group of officers planted a bomb on Hitler's plane during a visit to the Eastern Front in March 1943, but it failed to detonate. A second attempt was made a week later when Hitler attended an exhibition of captured Soviet weaponry in Berlin. It also failed.'

'But they kept trying, no?' Catherine asked.

'They did,' I confirmed. 'By mid-1943 it was clear to all but the most fanatical Nazis that the war was lost. The German offensive at Kursk had failed and the Western Allies had landed in Sicily. So General Henning von Tresckow and his fellow conspirators decided to try again. They were determined to kill Hitler and install an autocratic government that would be acceptable to the Western Allies. All in order to negotiate a separate peace that would prevent a Soviet invasion of Germany.'

Catherine shrugged. 'Well, they were right that the Nazis were a disaster for Germany.'

'Indeed,' I nodded. 'So, during the latter part of 1943 and early 1944, Tresckow and Stauffenberg tried at least five times to get one of their co-conspirators near enough to kill Hitler with hand grenades or a pistol. None of these plans were successful because, by this stage of the war, Hitler no longer appeared in public. He spent most of his time at his military headquarters in East Prussia with occasional breaks at the *Kehlsteinhaus*, his mountain retreat in Bavaria.'

'So, Hitler became a hermit?' asked Catherine.

'Sort of, I suppose. His paranoia had increased to the point where he rarely saw anyone beyond his personal circle of trust. The Gestapo was also suspicious of disloyalty within the army officer corps.'

'So, is that why they opted to use a time bomb? In July 1944 I mean.'

'Correct,' I confirmed. 'Tresckow and Stauffenberg thought it was the only option that would work. They were also living in constant fear of betrayal to the Gestapo. That's why they decided to go ahead with the plan to kill Hitler, even if it failed. They thought the world would see that there were people in Germany prepared to act against the Nazis.'

'Where did Himmler fit into all of this?' asked Catherine. 'He was head of the SS and Gestapo, after all.'

'Funny you should ask that,' I quipped. 'Himmler was content to leave the anti-Hitler resistance alone because he also realised that Germany was going to lose the war. Once Hitler was dead, he hoped to negotiate peace with the British and Americans.'

'Then he was both evil and stupid.'

I nodded. 'That's a fair way to put it. But Tresckow and the other army conspirators had no intention of removing Hitler just to see him replaced by the head of the SS. They planned to kill them both. In fact, Stauffenberg's initial assassination attempt on the 11th of July was aborted because Himmler wasn't present. The same thing happened three days later.'

'You mean they missed out on two chances to kill Hitler just because Himmler wasn't there as well?' Catherine exclaimed in wide-eyed disbelief.

'I'm afraid so,' I sighed. 'But there's more.'

'More?' she echoed.

I nodded. 'On the 15th of July, Stauffenberg flew to Hitler's command post in East Prussia carrying a briefcase bomb that he intended to plant in Hitler's conference room. After activating the timer, he would excuse himself, wait for the explosion and then fly back to Berlin.'

'In other words, the same plan they put into place on the 20th of July,' Catherine observed. 'What happened this time?'

'Himmler and Göring were there, but Hitler was called out of the room at the last moment – and Stauffenberg aborted…again.'

'I'm infuriated just listening to this,' Catherine said. 'I can only imagine how frustrated Tresckow and Stauffenberg must have been.'

'It wasn't just frustration they were feeling. On the 18th of July, they heard rumours that the Gestapo was onto them and that Stauffenberg might be arrested at any moment. This turned out not to be true, but at the time there was a sense the net was closing. They decided to seize on the next opportunity to kill Hitler, regardless.

'So, von Stauffenberg was a liberal democrat?'

I shook my head. 'Hardly. He was a hardcore German nationalist who had shown some sympathy for the Nazi Party during the early 1930s. But once Stauffenberg witnessed the atrocities inflicted by the SS and *Wehrmacht* in Poland and Russia, his attitude changed. He came to believe that the Nazis were staining the honour of Germany.'

'And what about Tresckow?' asked Catherine.

'There the picture is murkier.' I frowned. 'Tresckow showed no hesitation about deporting thousands of orphaned children to forced labour camps. I think he was more concerned about losing the war than with Nazi atrocities and war crimes.'

'He was an opportunist,' said Catherine.

I shrugged and went on. 'Some of the other conspirators were monarchists who wanted to reinstate Germany's 1914 boundaries with Belgium, France and Poland. Others yearned for a

German-dominated Europe, but they agreed on one demand…no reparations. They wanted a clean slate for Germany.'

'Do you think the Allies would have accepted these demands?'

'Of course not,' I declared. 'Remember the Allies issued their demand for unconditional surrender at the Casablanca Conference in January 1943. There was no way Roosevelt and Churchill would be willing to accept anything less.'

'Then how did the actual assassination attempt unfold on the day?' Catherine asked.

'Stauffenberg flew from Berlin to East Prussia on the Thursday morning – the 20th of July – with a bomb concealed in his briefcase. He was scheduled to provide a briefing at the *Wolfsschanze* on the readiness of the Home Army. A little after noon, Stauffenberg primed the bomb inside his briefcase and entered the conference room. He placed the briefcase beneath the table near where Hitler was standing. After several minutes, Stauffenberg was summoned to take a pre-arranged phone call and left the room.'

Catherine's brow furrowed. 'If the bomb was placed near Hitler, why wasn't he killed?'

'No one really knows for sure.' I shrugged. 'The prevailing theory is an officer named Colonel Brandt moved the briefcase behind the leg of the conference table, thereby deflecting the blast.'

'What happened to him?' asked Catherine.

'To Brandt? He lost a leg and died the next day. But he's a bit player in this drama. The bomb wounded more than twenty people. Hitler suffered a perforated eardrum and his clothes were singed, but he survived.'

'More's the pity,' sighed Catherine. 'Did Stauffenberg get away?'

'He saw the explosion and assumed that Hitler was dead. He climbed into a staff car, passed through three checkpoints and drove to the airfield. He was airborne and on his way to Berlin before anyone realised he was the one who planted the bomb.'

'What happened then?'

'By the time Stauffenberg landed at around 4 pm, news of Hitler's survival had reached the conspirators.'

'How big was the conspiracy and how many officers were involved?'

'No one knows, exactly. But the plan called for units of the Reserve Army to seize control of ministerial offices, radio stations and telephone exchanges in Berlin. This was codenamed Operation Valkyrie. And in some cases, that took place, but the plot collapsed that evening when Hitler telephoned Goebbels.'

Catherine's brow furrowed. 'But Goebbels was the propaganda minister. How was a spin doctor able to crush a coup attempt?'

'The commander of the Berlin security battalion was an officer named Otto Remer. Major Remer was told by General Paul von Hase, one of the anti-Hitler conspirators, that Hitler was dead and was ordered to arrest Goebbels. However, when Remer arrived at the Propaganda Ministry, Goebbels informed the major that Hitler survived the assassination attempt. The major demanded proof whereupon Goebbels placed a call to the *Wolfsshanze*, and Remer spoke to Hitler. Realising that he'd been taking orders from conspirators, Remer moved his troops to Berlin military headquarters and arrested Stauffenberg and the other plotters.'

'My God!' spat Catherine. 'Are you telling me the plot failed just because this one major was loyal to Hitler?'

I shook my head. 'Not really. I think Hitler's survival doomed the conspiracy to failure. There's no way the German army would have sided with the conspirators so long as the Führer remained alive. Remember, they had taken oaths of allegiance to Hitler as a person. But the most contemptible figure in the whole affair was Friedrich Fromm.'

'Who was he?' asked Catherine.

'Fromm was commander of the Reserve Army.'

'You mean he was Stauffenberg's direct commander?'

'Yes,' I confirmed. 'He was aware of the Valkyrie plot but tried to play both sides. He did nothing to stop the conspiracy, but moved to execute Stauffenberg and the other conspirators once it became clear that Hitler had survived – and that landed him in big trouble.'

'Why?' asked Catherine. 'You would think that the Nazis would be appreciative of such decisive action.'

'Put it this way…when Fromm tried to take credit for snuffing out the conspiracy, Goebbels was reported to have said, "You were in a damned hurry to put all the witnesses underground."'

'They suspected him of involvement in the plot,' mused Catherine. 'But was he involved?'

'Fromm was a fence-sitter who tried to play both sides, but it didn't help.'

'The Nazis killed him anyway?'

'Oh yes,' I nodded. 'They tossed him into prison and shot him just before the end of the war, but he was just one among thousands.'

'What do you mean?' Catherine asked.

'Over the following weeks, the Gestapo rounded up nearly everyone who had any connection with the coup plotters. They discovered letters and diaries in the homes and offices of those arrested that revealed the failed coups of 1938, 1939 and 1943.'

'Which led to further arrests?'

'Precisely,' I agreed. 'The Gestapo cast a very wide net and not everyone arrested was involved in the 20th of July conspiracy. But the Nazis saw this as an opportunity to settle scores with many others suspected of opposition sympathies.'

'Was there any sort of due process in all this?' Catherine asked quietly.

'Hardly,' I scoffed. 'The Nazis held show trials that were filmed for propaganda purposes. The military officers among the conspirators were court-martialled and expelled from the army.

They were then tried by a so-called People's Court where the presiding judge was Roland Friesler, the thug I mentioned.'

'When did the trials take place?' Catherine asked, her voice tight.

'The first trials were held on the 7th and 8th of August 1944. Hitler ordered that those found guilty should be hanged, but some of the accused beat the hangman by taking their own lives.'

Catherine shrugged but said nothing.

'Tresckow killed himself with a hand grenade the day after the assassination. Before pulling the pin he reportedly said: "I am convinced we did the right thing. Hitler is the enemy of Germany and the world."'

'I read somewhere that the Pope was involved,' said Catherine. 'Is this true?'

'Good question,' I replied. 'A report by SS General Ernst Kaltenbrunner stated that, at the very least, Pope Pius XII knew about the coup.'

Catherine sat looking at me across my desk with a pensive expression on her face. 'Papa, you said earlier that Hitler believed *Opa* was involved in the coup attempt. Was he right?'

'We don't know,' I sighed. 'I've looked into that question and opinions are mixed. Some historians say my father supported the coup, but not Hitler's assassination. Others say he knew about the conspiracy and wanted Hitler arrested and placed on trial.'

'Did you ever discuss it with *Oma*?'

'On her deathbed, she told me that *Opa* believed an attempt on Hitler's life could trigger a civil war.'

Catherine looked solemn. 'So why did Hitler believe *Opa* was party to the coup?'

I shrugged. 'Apparently some of the conspirators said that *Opa* agreed Hitler had to be removed for the sake of Germany.'

'But weren't those confessions obtained under torture?' she demanded.

'True,' I said, 'but the Gestapo discovered written plans drawn up by the conspirators in which *Opa* was to become a member of the post-Hitler government.'

'But just because *Opa's* name was mentioned doesn't mean he knew about it,' Catherine protested.

'That's right,' I agreed. 'But from our perspective wouldn't you prefer it if he was involved? Wouldn't that have been the more honourable thing?'

Catherine sat in silence for several moments before nodding. 'You're right. I never thought about it like that.'

'Not so simple after all,' I said.

'In some ways maybe,' she agreed.

'Your *oma* told me that *Opa* lost faith in Hitler in 1943 when he learned what was happening to the Jews – the death camps, slave labour…She said he lost confidence in Germany's ability to win the war. That was when he met the conspirators who wanted to oust Hitler.'

Catherine frowned.

'In the reprisals that followed the failed attempt on Hitler's life, *Opa's* defeatist attitude to the war would have enraged Hitler.'

'Of course.'

'The problem for Hitler was how to eliminate Germany's most popular general without revealing to the people that he had ordered his death.'

'So, what did he do?'

'He decided to force *Opa* to commit suicide.'

'I can't imagine what that must have been like for *Opa* and the family,' Catherine said, dismayed.

'I was only fifteen, but even so I was part of an anti-aircraft crew – the Führer demanded a lot of the Hitler Youth. I was lucky I didn't end up on the front line, like some boys my age. They gave me leave to go home and visit my father.'

'So, at least you got to see him.'

'We all knew that your *opa* was under suspicion after the failed attempt. They'd arrested his chief of staff and his commanding officer.'

'*Oma* and the family must have feared the worst for *Opa*.'

'When I arrived home your *opa* was eating breakfast. I joined him and then we walked in the garden. "At twelve o'clock two generals are coming to discuss my future employment," he told me. At that stage I think he was still not sure what was about to happen to him.'

'So, what did happen?'

'Around midday, a dark-green car pulled up outside our garden gate. Two generals got out and went into the house. They weren't rude. They asked my father's permission to speak to him alone quite politely. I left them to it.'

Catherine hesitated, looked at me for a long moment, 'And then…?'

'*Well, at least they are not going to arrest him*, I thought.'

'But…?'

'After a few minutes I heard my father go upstairs and into my mother's room. I followed him, anxious to know what was happening. He was standing there, his face pale, and when he heard me he turned and said in a tight voice, "Come with me." I followed him into my room. "I have just told your mother that I shall be dead in a quarter of an hour." He continued calmly, "Hitler is charging me with treason. I am to die by poison. The two generals have brought it with them. It's fatal in minutes. If I accept, none of the usual steps will be taken against you and the family."'

'"Do you believe them?" I said.'

'"Yes," he replied. "It is in their interest to see that none of this comes out. You must promise to remain absolutely silent. If you breathe a word of this to anyone, they will no longer be bound by the agreement."'

'So, what did you do?' Catherine said, blinking anxiously.

'I was scared. My father had just placed the fate of my family in my hands, and for a long time, I didn't speak. Then your *opa* said in a thin voice, "It's better for one of us to die than for all of us to be shot." He hesitated for a moment, then with a wry smile said, "Besides, we have almost no ammunition, and they have the place surrounded."'

'"Oh Papa—" I began, but he gripped my arm hard and said dryly, "I'm to be given a state funeral. In a quarter of an hour, they'll telephone my aide from the *Wagnerschule* reserve hospital in Ulm to say that I've had a brain seizure on the way to a conference." Then he looked at his watch. "I must go, they've only given me ten minutes." We embraced hurriedly and went downstairs together.'

Catherine's eyes filled with tears. She stared at me in disbelief. 'How could he be so calm?' she said almost to herself. 'What courage.'

'As your *opa* went into the hall, his little dachshund jumped up at him with a cry of joy. "Shut the dog in the study, Manfred," my father said, and waited in the hall while I removed the excited puppy and pushed it through the study door. Then we walked out of the house together. The two generals were waiting by the garden gate. We walked slowly down the path towards them, and I noticed everything, as if it were exaggerated. Even the crunch of the gravel sounded unnaturally loud.'

'That must have been awful!'

'As we approached, the generals saluted. "Herr Field Marshal," they said and stood aside for your *opa* to pass through the gate. A group of villagers stood outside watching. I felt myself beginning to sweat. The SS driver opened the door and stood to attention. My father slipped his marshal's baton under his arm, and calmly shook my hand and stepped into the car.'

A crimson flush spread across Catherine's face and she blinked hurriedly.

'The two generals then climbed into the car and shut the doors. My father did not look back as the car drove off up the hill and disappeared round a bend. When it had gone, I turned and walked silently back into the house.'

'My God, what an ordeal for you and *Oma* to go through, not to mention poor *Opa*!'

'Twenty minutes later the telephone rang and the person on the line told us that *Opa* was dead.'

Catherine looked dazed.

'Later we heard that the car had stopped a few hundred yards up the hill at the edge of the wood. The Gestapo were watching the area with instructions to shoot my father and storm the house if he resisted in any way. The driver got out of the car, leaving my father inside. When the driver returned ten minutes later, he saw my father slumped forward with his cap off and the marshal's baton fallen from his hand.'

'You must have grieved for your father,' Catherine said.

'It was the end for me. I deserted and then surrendered to the French. What was the point of fighting for such barbarians who could do that to my father?'

She shrugged. 'But you made sure he was remembered for all the right reasons. You helped to establish museums honouring him, and you became friends with the children of his enemies, the sons of General Patton and Field Marshall Montgomery. If that isn't a symbol of postwar Anglo-German reconciliation I don't know what is…'

'You're making me blush.' I gave her a shaky smile. 'Let's keep our focus on *Opa*, dear Catherine. Today most Germans view the Valkyrie conspirators as heroes. I'd like to think *Opa* was one of them.'

I have drawn heavily on the article 'The Forced Suicide of Field Marshall Rommel, 1944', and gratefully acknowledge it: EyeWitness to History, 2002, http://www.eyewitnesstohistory.com/rommel.htm

The Warsaw Ghetto Uprising

'Thank you for inviting me, Mrs Silverman,' I said, proffering a bottle of red wine purchased the day before at the kosher supermarket on Glen Huntly Road.

'It's our pleasure.'

Hannah Silverman was a slender woman in her fifties and the evening's host. 'After all, you're a nice Jewish girl studying here in Melbourne all alone. That means you're in need of a good home-cooked Shabbat meal. Especially with Pesach coming.'

I just smiled, deciding that discretion was the best response when it came to any mention of my irreligious Upper East Side New York Jewish family. I suppose the best way to describe us would be cultural Jews. Or 'three-fers', a term I once heard that was used to describe those who showed up at synagogue only on Rosh Hashanah, Yom Kippur and Passover. My parents were American progressives who looked to *The New York Times* for guidance, rather than the Torah. So, some things were probably best left unsaid.

'We are also privileged to have at our table tonight my eldest cousin, Ya'akov Zeigler, along with his wife Channah, who are visiting us from Israel. And I also want to welcome our other guests, Etty's parents, Moshe and Rachel.'

A pleasant pine scent pervaded the house, emanating from a stocky yellow candle that burned on the mantelpiece.

A portly man in his fifties approached. I saw he wore a knitted *kippah* atop his balding head. 'I'm Hershel, Hannah's husband. Welcome to our home. Sit anywhere you like.'

'Thank you so much for your hospitality,' I replied, sliding into the nearest chair, which was midway down the long dinner table. Around me people were taking their seats.

Hershel tapped his spoon on the Kiddush glass and gazed at his guests in expectant silence as the room fell quiet. 'It's lovely to see everyone. We have three generations of friends and family assembled in one home. That alone is a living triumph over *Tzorerai Yisrael* – the oppressors of the Jewish people.'

He nodded in my direction. 'And our lovely guests from America and Israel, of course.'

I blushed as all eyes turned to me. 'Hi, I'm Anna Lushkin from New York. I'm here doing my MBA at Melbourne University. Thank you very much for the invitation and thanks to AUJS...the Jewish student organisation on campus, for connecting me to the Silverman family.'

A bookish young man in his late twenties or early thirties smiled at me. 'I'm Aaron Silverman, Hershel's son. And this is my wife Etty.'

The pretty dark-haired woman seated beside him pointed towards a cot in the corner. 'Don't forget our little Amalia.'

I rose from the table for a quick peek at the sleeping infant. 'She's gorgeous,' I cooed. 'How old?'

'Four months,' replied Etty, her face glowing with maternal pride.

'Lovely to meet you,' I replied.

A slender, bespectacled man in his seventies with a head crowned by a thick shock of silver hair sat quietly without joining the round of introductions. I waved and received a sombre smile in reply.

Over my four undergraduate years at Swarthmore College, I attended more than a few Shabbat dinners at the campus Hillel House. So, I was familiar with the sequence of blessings and rituals: the lighting of candles, followed by the Kiddush over the wine and ceremonial washing of hands.

After everyone retook their seats with cleansed hands, Hershel reached forward and removed the ornate doily on the table to reveal two loaves of braided challah egg bread. Using a serrated knife, he cut the challah into small squares and distributed it to the seated guests.

'*Baruch atah Adonai, Eloheynu Melech Haolam, ha motzei lechem min ha'aretz,*' he intoned before taking a bite of bread.

'Amen,' the guests echoed in unison.

Hershel gestured towards the platters heaped high with chicken, roast beef and vegetables. 'I now invite you to dig in with good appetite. Once you've eaten there'll be a treat in store.'

Over the next twenty-five minutes, conversation competed with the delicious food that was available in abundance.

After dessert was cleared away and the dinner attendees were sitting around the table with satisfied expressions, Hershel tapped his wine glass with a fork.

'*Gut* Shabbat, everyone. As you know, this is Shabbat *Hagadol*, the final Shabbat before Pesach…the Passover holiday. Passover is a celebration of our liberation as a people over four thousand years ago.

'But this Pesach of *Taf Shin Samech Gimel* – the year 5063 in the Hebrew calendar – also marks the anniversary of another Jewish struggle for freedom. Sixty years ago, a handful of brave young Jews rose up against the Nazi regime that was murdering our people. Armed only with pistols, homemade grenades, a few rifles and a couple of machineguns, these Jews were completely outmatched by the SS.'

Hershel paused and sent a glance of silent appraisal around the room, nodding in satisfaction at the rapt expressions he saw around him.

'Despite the hopelessness of their cause, these Jewish fighters – men and women alike – fought on. Not with any expectation of victory. It was simply out of a desire to die on their feet with dignity, rather than go as passive victims to the slaughter. We are privileged to have at our table tonight one of those heroes, my cousin Ya'akov Zeigler, who is visiting us from Israel along with his wife Channah.'

Hershel indicated the quiet, silver-haired guest who I saw was seated beside his heavy-set wife of a similar age.

'In 1943, when he was just fifteen years old, Ya'akov took part in the Warsaw Ghetto Uprising as part of the Jewish Military Association, one of the two Jewish militias who fought the Germans. He was one of the few who survived – to be smuggled out of the city through the sewers.

'He spent the rest of the war as a partisan fighting in the Białowieża Forest. Deciding that Europe was nothing more than a massive Jewish graveyard, he made his way along *Aliya Bet* smuggling routes to Italy where he boarded a Haganah ship that would try to run the British naval blockade of Eretz Yisrael.'

'Excuse me, but what was the *Aliya Bet*?' I asked.

'The campaign to smuggle Jewish Holocaust survivors past the British navy blockade into Israel,' replied Hershel.

'Like in the book *Exodus*?'

'Yes, and the movie,' said the silver-haired Ya'akov, his eyes alight with a mischievous smile. 'In those days, I was even better-looking than Paul Newman.'

Everyone at the table – including me – doubled over as a gale of laughter swept the room.

'Anyway,' continued Hershel after regaining his composure, 'Ya'akov's ship was intercepted by the Royal Navy and he was sent to a detention camp in Cyprus. And that's where he met Channah.'

Channah Zeigler blushed as a shy smile flashed across her face. 'After the State of Israel was created, Ya'akov and Channah made Aliyah to Israel and he fought in the War of Independence. He later studied law at the Hebrew University and went on to a career as a lawyer, and then magistrate. Having reached the mandatory retirement age, Ya'akov and Channah have embarked on a tour of the world. They have four children and thirteen grandchildren.'

'So far,' smiled Ya'akov, triggering another eruption of titters around the table.

'I'll stop here,' said Hershel. 'I think it's pretty clear that Ya'akov can tell his own story. So, rather than me relating it second-hand, you'll find it more interesting to hear from the man who lived through it. Ya'akov?'

'Well, Hershel, I certainly wasn't expecting this,' smiled Ya'akov, his fluent English tinged with a strong Polish accent. 'So, I don't know whether I should thank you or curse you.'

He paused to allow the laughter of his audience to subside. 'But I suppose I'm now on the spot.'

'Please continue,' implored Etty. 'It would be a privilege to hear your story.'

Ya'akov nodded. 'I was born in 1928, the youngest of four children. My father was a professor of orthopaedic surgery at the Medical University of Warsaw and my mother kept one of the city's most fashionable social salons. Of my entire family, I am the only one to survive the war. My two sisters, my brother and my parents were all murdered by the Germans and their Polish collaborators.'

He sighed, and paused to remove his glasses and wipe a tear from his eye as the mood around the table darkened.

'My parents were Revisionist Zionists. Followers of Jabotinsky. They planned to emigrate to Eretz Yisrael during the 1930s, but there was a strict immigration quota for Jews imposed by the British. So, we were still stuck in Warsaw when the Germans invaded.'

'Damn the British and their White Paper,' muttered Moshe, an older man, perhaps in his seventies.

Ya'akov shrugged. 'In April 1940, the Germans forced Jewish men into working parties to build a wall around a designated area in the middle of Warsaw. By November the wall encompassed an area of over three square kilometres. The ghetto.'

'For local reference, that's just slightly larger than Elsternwick,' added Hershel.

'The Nazis crammed almost half a million people into the ghetto. The six of us shared one room with two other families. Fifteen people living in a space two-thirds the size of this one.'

'If "living" can be used to describe such conditions,' snorted Hannah.

Another shrug from Ya'akov. 'Of course, disease ran rampant. We became used to the sight of the dead being carted through the streets in wheelbarrows. By mid-1942 over 90,000 ghetto residents had died from typhus and malnutrition.'

'Did the Germans provide any food at all?' asked Aaron.

'Official rations accounted for a few hundred calories per day,' shrugged Ya'akov. 'One-tenth of a healthy adult diet. So we smuggled in what food we could get on the outside.'

'How did that work?' asked Hershel.

'There was a flourishing black market on the gentile side of the wall. Children were the best smugglers because we were small enough to squeeze through gaps in the wall or the sewers.'

'Wasn't that dangerous?' I asked.

'Oh yes,' nodded Ya'akov. 'There were summary executions almost daily. Anyone caught trying to cross the wall was put up against the nearest wall and shot. We were desperate. People sold whatever valuables they had for food, but it was never enough. My parents…'

Ya'akov's voice cracked and I saw his Adam's apple bob up and down. He swallowed in an effort to maintain his composure.

'My parents were the first to go. Momma died, followed a month later by my father. They kept giving us most of whatever food we managed to acquire. We watched them waste away before our eyes.'

'Bastards,' I muttered as my eyes began to prick with tears.

Ya'akov graced me with a sad smile. 'Yes, they were, and most of the Poles were little better. There were a few righteous people who risked their lives to save Jewish lives. But antisemitism in Poland was rife at that time.'

'Today as well,' interjected Hannah Silverman. 'Look at the current Polish government's law against Holocaust restitution.'

'Oh yes,' agreed Ya'akov. 'There were many Poles who were quite happy to take possession of empty Jewish homes and businesses. But the Germans were impatient. Starvation and disease weren't doing the job quickly enough. So in July 1942, the deportations began. People were ordered to assemble for resettlement at the *Umschlagplatz* on Mila Street next to the railyard.'

'That was just a ploy, wasn't it?' asked Hershel.

'Exactly so. In the beginning, people were convinced by the stories of work camps with good food and living conditions.

But then we saw what happened when they showed up at the *Umschlagplatz*…the assembly area. They were set upon by German troops and the ghetto police, and forced into cattle cars. Then we received reports about what was happening at Treblinka.'

'What were you told?' I asked. 'And by whom?'

'I was a member of the Jewish Military Association, the ŻZW. I'll talk more about the resistance groups later. But one of our members had a railway-worker friend and managed to slip aboard the locomotive of a train leaving the ghetto. The railwaymen told him that up to six trains arrived at Treblinka each day. All of them packed with thousands of Jews. When the trains left Treblinka, they were empty. Our man could see no barracks for so many people. There were no wells to supply drinking water and no supplies of food delivered. Then there was the stench.'

'Aah,' gasped Etty, her hand rising to cover her mouth as Aaron slipped a comforting arm around her shoulders.

'The camp was surrounded by a barbed-wire fence with pine branches interwoven between the strands to obscure lines of sight. He could see the tops of several smokestacks that were belching black clouds into the sky. He returned to report that the resettlement story was a lie. That the trains were delivering our friends, neighbours and family to a death factory.'

'You mentioned the ghetto police. Who were they?' I asked.

'They were scum who worked as enforcers for the Germans,' Ya'akov snorted, his mouth curled in contempt. 'Low-life Jews who sold out their people for a bit of extra food and special privileges.'

'So they were like *Kapos*?' asked Hannah Silverman.

'Just as bad,' Ya'akov growled. 'A handful joined to work as double agents for the resistance. But most of them were just *mamzers*. The lowest of the low.'

'So, once you found out what was happening at Treblinka, you began to organise the resistance?' asked Hershel.

Ya'akov shook his head. 'Our group, ŻZW, was organised in November 1939. It was led by several Jewish officers in the Polish army and most of the fighters were recruited from Beitar, the conservative Zionist youth group founded by Jabotinsky.'

'But wasn't there another underground group?' Aaron asked.

'Yes,' nodded Ya'akov, 'the ŻOB, the Jewish Combat Organisation. They came into being later. In 1942.'

'Why so late?' I asked.

'There are several theories,' Ya'akov replied. 'I tend to think that it's because of Hitler's alliance with Stalin.'

'The Molotov–Ribbentrop Pact?' I asked.

'That's the one. You see, the members of the ŻOB came from two left-wing Zionist movements, the socialist Habonin Dror and the Marxist Hashomer Hatzair. There are those who believe that the Jewish Left didn't want to rock the boat while Germany and the Soviet Union were allies. Of course, the survivors of those groups deny this, but it's a view that I share. At this point, the issue is rather moot, anyway. What's important is that once we learned what was happening at Treblinka, our two underground militia groups began working together.'

'How did you get weapons?' asked Aaron.

'By hook and by crook. We stole them, bought them on the black market. Our group, the ŻZW, was led by former Polish army officers, so we used their personal connections to acquire weapons and explosives from the Armia Krajowa…the Polish Home Army. We were better armed than the socialists of the ŻOB, but still, we didn't have nearly enough. Six machine guns, around twenty submachine guns, fifty rifles and fifty pistols. A few hundred homemade grenades.'

'Not much against the might of the German army,' I murmured.

'You don't understand, my dear,' said Ya'akov, 'we had no expectation of victory. We simply wanted to kill as many Germans as possible before going to our deaths with dignity. The fact that I'm alive amazes me even after sixty years.'

'So did you and the ŻOB work together?'

Ya'akov nodded. 'I once read a quote by Benjamin Franklin who warned the American rebels against Britain that "if we don't hang together, we'll all hang separately". And when weighed against what the Germans were doing, the differences between our conservative Zionist philosophy and their socialist Zionist viewpoint seemed insignificant. So we joined forces and in January 1943 Mordechai Anielewicz led our first armed action.'

'Kibbutz Yad Mordechai is named after him, no?' asked Aaron.

'Yes, it is. Anielewicz began as a member of the ŻZW, but the ŻOB offered him the leadership role in 1942. So he went over to them.'

'What was this first action?' prompted Hershel.

'It happened in January 1943. By this stage over half of the ghetto's population had already been deported, but during that first wave we didn't have the weapons to intervene. Once the second mass roundup was announced we weren't going to wait any longer.'

Ya'akov paused for a moment to polish his glasses before forging on with the story that held everyone's rapt attention.

'On January eighteenth, a group of a dozen fighters from both resistance movements spread among the crowd at the *Umschlagplatz* – the assembly point near the railway line where people were loaded onto trains. Our people opened fire with pistols on the SS guards and ghetto police, killing over a dozen. Most of these resistance fighters paid with their lives to enable thousands of Jews to escape the roundup back into the ghetto. This was the opening salvo, so to speak, in the uprising.'

'How did the Germans react?' I asked, despite dreading to hear the answer.

'Three days later they rounded up and shot one thousand Jews. But the deportations stopped for a time.'

'The uprising itself began on the first night of Passover, didn't it?' asked Etty. 'So, what did you do between January and April?'

Ya'akov smiled. 'We dug bunkers and connecting tunnels. We continued to beg, buy and steal weapons and ammunition. We trained as best we could. I was issued a Luger pistol and fifty bullets. It was my pride and joy. I would practise for hours in the cellars, disassembling and assembling the pistol and dry firing. There wasn't enough ammunition for live fire training, so the first bullet I ever shot was into the back of an SS trooper on the first day of the revolt.'

'A good day,' I said, surprising myself with my bloodthirsty vengefulness.

'It was a good feeling,' nodded Ya'akov.

'We delivered justice to every collaborator we could lay our hands on. Ghetto police and officials of the *Judenraat*…the Jewish ghetto government. And every informer who was lurking around the streets. We held trials and carried out death sentences.'

'And rightly so,' I found myself saying indignantly.

'So by mid-April 1943 we were as ready as we'd ever be,' Ya'akov continued. 'We had about seven hundred fighters. Men and women, teenage boys and girls. I'd just had my fifteenth birthday and some of our fighters were younger than me.'

'How terrible,' gasped Etty.

Ya'akov shrugged. 'Desperate times. We knew that the Germans were about to restart the deportations to Treblinka. So we warned all remaining Jews in the ghetto to take shelter in the bunkers we'd built. Shortly after midday on April nineteenth, a column of SS and *Ordnungspolizei* marched through the main gate of the ghetto as if on a parade ground. We were waiting for them.'

Ya'akov paused to sip from a glass of mineral water.

'We were there to show them a new type of Jew. A Jew who was prepared to kill and unafraid to die. This was something they'd never before encountered. Their arrogance turned to panic when we opened fire. They scattered like scalded rabbits. It was a glorious sight to behold.'

'How many of them did you manage to kill that first day?' asked Aaron, smiling.

Ya'akov looked at him in earnest. 'I got one. In total, we killed twenty-seven and wounded another thirty-two, with only seven casualties on our side. When the Germans returned later that afternoon for a second try, they brought two armoured vehicles that we destroyed with petrol bombs thrown from the rooftops.'

'Poetic justice,' I said, 'burning the Nazis who were coming to burn Jews.'

'Yes,' agreed Ya'akov, 'that's an irony that we recognised. But after that first day, things became harder. The Germans were no longer goosestepping, but advancing in tactical formation. They brought up artillery to destroy any building we were firing from. They used flamethrowers to burn us out. I'll never forget the petrol stench of the flames and the smell of burning flesh. To this day I can't refuel our car. Channah has to do it.'

Channah Ziegler leaned over and took her husband's hand in hers.

'So it went, day by day, house by house and block by block. The Germans pushed us back until by late April we were surrounded in a four-block area around the ŻZW command bunker on Muranówska Street. That meant we were separated from the remnants of the ŻOB, who were fighting around their command bunker at number eighteen Mila Street.'

'So, what did you do?' I asked, utterly enthralled by this story.

Ya'akov shrugged. 'We fought. One of our strongholds at seven Muranówska Street was just across from the ghetto wall. There was a tunnel that we'd dug to the gentile side of the city and we received supplies of ammunition from the Polish Home Army – but there was never enough. By early May, we were down to a couple of dozen fighters with almost no ammunition. Paweł Frenkiel and most of our other commanders were dead. So we decided to break out through the Muranówska tunnel on the night of May third, but even that didn't go to plan.'

'What happened?' gasped Etty.

'Betrayal.' Ya'akov grimaced. 'One of the Polish resistance men who was supposed to guide us turned out to be a double agent. He led us into an ambush. We had to fight our way through. Those of us who survived made our way to the Kampinoski Forest. We travelled in a horse-drawn cart owned by a sympathetic local – we were fortunate.

'And when we got there we joined a unit of partisans. We later heard that Anielewicz and the last remnants of the ŻOB committed suicide at the eighteen Mila Street bunker, rather than surrender.'

Ya'akov stopped for a long moment before announcing in a sombre voice, 'That's my story of the Warsaw Ghetto Uprising.'

'So tragic,' Etty said, her voice trembling.

'So much courage,' I murmured.

Hershel stood up from his seat at the head of the table. 'Thank you so much for sharing your story. It's been a privilege to listen to you. If anyone thinks others might be interested, Ya'akov will be speaking at our shul's Kiddush lunch following the Shabbat morning service tomorrow morning.'

'Which shul is this?' I asked.

Hershel smiled at my question. 'Young Israel on Inkerman Street. It's just around the corner. Now please join me as we *bensch*. You should each have a prayer book with the blessing after the food.'

I picked up the Hebrew-only booklet and turned to the first page, striving to keep up with my bat mitzva–level grasp of the right-to-left text.

'Shir hama'alot beshuva Adonai et shivat Ziyon hayeenu ke'cholmim…'

I was soon left behind as the others thumbed their way through the 600-plus words of the blessing.

Then, after thanking my hosts, it was time to take my leave. But not before receiving an invitation to the Silverman family Passover Seder that coming Wednesday evening.

I came away from that Shabbat evening meal feeling happy, but unsettled. Of course, I knew of the Holocaust, having taken a course in college and endured Sunday school lessons at my reform synagogue. But my great-grandparents moved to the United States during the great wave of Jewish emigration from Tzarist Russia at the turn of the twentieth century. So, while I certainly knew there were members of my family who perished at Nazi hands, the links were rendered too tenuous by time and geography to give that catastrophe a human face. Until now.

That night was the first time I came face to face with someone who had actually been there. A hero, no less. My grand plan was to combine my Australian MBA with my American BA and embark on a career in international business management. As the days passed, I began to wonder. The fact that I had never visited Israel became an itch I just had to scratch. So, the next stop on my global mystery tour was the Hebrew University. There I completed a specialised masters in entrepreneurship and innovation. After all, where better to study such things than the famous 'start-up' nation?

To cut a long story short, that's where I met a remarkable man named Alon who became my husband.

So, in a way, it all began at the Shabbat dinner table in Melbourne. Half a world away, with a Jewish husband and three Jewish children, I feel as though I'm doing my bit to repair the world from the catastrophe visited upon my people by the Third Reich.

The Secret Stain

Emily glanced at the waiter who stood behind her right shoulder. He tugged at the cork of a 2001 Dalwhinnie Moonambel Shiraz, then poured a fifth into her glass. After swirling the purple-crimson liquid, she inhaled the scent of dark berries and spice before taking a mouthful.

'Hmm, it's good,' she sighed. 'You can leave the bottle, thanks.'

Emily and Joanne sat opposite each other at their favourite local bar overlooking Elwood Beach. It was a dull, cold Sunday in late August and the fresh air had brought the colour to their cheeks. Each of them felt life was better with the other in it. The love they shared was obvious in their ready smiles and long adoring looks. They chatted, picked at the canapés, sipped wine, held hands and watched the fishermen on the pier with their lines in the water. Jet skis roared by offshore, much to the dismay of the fishermen who gestured frantically to the riders to leave.

Emily was a tall woman in her late twenties with penetrating dark eyes and blonde hair pulled back from her oval face in a tight ponytail. She projected confidence. Her brown eyes seemed to assess her interlocutors with a look. She had recently completed her PhD in politics at Monash University and was now a tenure-track lecturer in the history department at LaTrobe.

Joanne's eyes were blue, her face long, her mouth wide. Gentle and kind in disposition, which Emily found endearing, she was not afraid to speak her mind. Joanne was an aspiring poet, having graduated from Monash with an English degree. From their first meeting at the Main Dining Room at the Monash Campus Centre, Joanne had felt a connection that was almost electric. Sometimes she felt she was put on this earth for no reason other than to be with Emily.

Now she reached for her water and sipped to clear her throat. 'What are you reading at the moment?' she asked. 'Anything I'd like?'

'It's an article by Annie Jacobsen about Operation Paperclip.' Emily paused to sip her wine.

'Never heard of it.'

'It was a secret US intelligence program put in place after the war,' Emily replied. 'Between 1945 and 1959, the CIA moved more than sixteen hundred German scientists, engineers and technicians to the US.'

'Really?' asked Joanne.

'Really,' echoed Emily. 'And many of them were former members of the Nazi Party. Some were even members of the SS.'

'That's disgusting!' Joanne snorted. 'Why would they do that?'

Emily shrugged. 'Because of the Cold War. The Germans had developed superior jet-engine and missile technology. The Americans wanted to preserve their advantage over the Russians. But they were doing it too.'

'Who's they?' asked Joanne. 'The Russians?'

'Yep,' nodded Emily. 'In 1946, Stalin moved over two thousand German scientists and engineers along with six thousand of their family members to research facilities in Russia.'

'So it was all about the Cold War,' mused Joanne.

'You got it,' Emily confirmed. 'It all started just a couple of months after the end of the war in Europe. The US military organised Operation Overcast, a secret recruitment program designed to help shorten the war in the Pacific. The Germans were the first ones to use jet aircraft and ballistic missiles in combat. They were way ahead of American and British technology. Then, when Japan surrendered, the name of the game was staying ahead of the Russians.'

Joanne shook her head in disgust. 'That's appalling. Think about the survivors of the Holocaust and their relatives. Imagine how they must have felt – the pain it must have caused them.'

'They didn't know,' replied Emily. 'At least not in the beginning. It was a top-secret operation. But later, the press interviewed several scientists and started asking questions. The Pentagon then began to peddle the line that these were "good" Germans. Of course, that was total bullshit.'

'Jesus, Mother of Christ,' Joanne muttered and bit her lower lip.

'Not what those Holocaust survivors would say, but I agree with the sentiment,' said Emily. 'So once the Pacific war was over, in November 1945, Operation Overcast was renamed Operation Paperclip. The name was derived from the paperclips attached to the folders of rocket experts that America sought to recruit.'

'Did President Truman know about this? I thought he was sympathetic to the Jews. He recognised Israel when it declared independence in 1948, didn't he?'

Emily sighed. 'Not only did he know about it, but he formally approved it. He authorised an expansion of Operation Paperclip to take in another one thousand German scientists.'

'How do you know all this?' asked Joanne, disgust and shock apparent in her voice.

'I'm teaching it this semester.'

'What is it about Americans?' Joanne said. 'What sort of morality do they have that they think it's okay to protect Nazi war criminals? Is it any wonder that a morally bankrupt person like Donald Trump can be elected president? They live in Disneyland. They're openly hostile to anyone who is different from them, they have contempt for reputable news outlets, and they embrace the redistribution of wealth to those who have it at the continued expense of those who don't.'

Emily smiled and raised her glass and a corresponding smile spread across Joanne's face. Emily touched the tip of her tongue to her upper lip, and feeling Joanne's hand on her knee, she leaned in for a kiss.

'I remember how you tasted last night,' murmured Joanne with a shy smile. 'I can't remember ever being so taken by anyone.'

Emily smiled her Cheshire cat smile.

'I mean it,' Joanne repeated.

'I know,' said Emily. 'So do I.'

'But I want to hear more about Operation Paperclip,' Joanne continued after a long pause.

'Okay,' said Emily. 'Well, after Stalingrad, it became clear that Germany was unable to defeat the Soviets. So, by early 1943, the German government began to recall scientists, engineers and technicians from combat to do research to bolster its weapons research programs. Just before the end of the war, a Polish laboratory assistant at the University of Bonn found a list of those scientists' names stuffed down a toilet. He passed it on to British intelligence which, in turn, gave it to the US military.'

'In a toilet?' giggled Joanne, her hand covering her mouth.

'In a toilet,' echoed Emily. 'A major in US army intelligence sent a message up the chain of command recommending the evacuation of these scientists and their families to America. He thought they could be of help in the war effort against Japan. So in July 1945, the American military began to move German rocket engineers to the US.'

'Like Wernher von Braun?'

'Yes,' replied Emily. 'I'm impressed you know his name.'

'I'm a big Tom Lehrer fan,' grinned Joanne. '"Vonce de rockets are up, who cares vere dey come down. Dat's not my department says Wernher von Braun."'

Emily struggled to contain a giggle. 'It's no laughing matter,' she said, trying to look stern.

'Right,' nodded Joanne with a twinkle in her eye. 'Sorry.'

'So the US then created something they called the Combined Intelligence Objectives Subcommittee. It targeted scientific, military and industrial personnel who could contribute to American technology. It was also tasked with finding out what technology the Germans may have passed on to Japan. They tried to prevent the emigration of German scientists to places like Spain, Argentina or Egypt, all of which had sympathised with Nazi Germany. It was all about getting their hands on these scientists before the Russians could get them, or they could scarper off to South America.'

'There are many things in this world I don't understand,' Joanne said with a grimace. 'And one of them is how the US could do such a thing. It's morally bankrupt.'

Emily shrugged. 'That's America for you. By 1947, they netted over 1,500 technicians and scientists and almost 4,000 of their family members. They were taken to villages in the German countryside and provided with stipends. In return, they had to report twice weekly to the local police station.'

Joanne sipped her wine.

'They were in limbo until November 1947, when the US held a conference to consider their status. Some of them filed monetary claims against the United States over their detention and possible American violations of the Geneva Convention.'

'The nerve of those arseholes!' Joanne spat. 'By rights they should have been tried at Nuremberg for war crimes. Yet they turn around and sue because they're being kept in country villas?'

'Outrageous, I agree,' nodded Emily. 'And some more cynical voices have argued that Operation Paperclip was a great success because it deprived Germany of its best minds for three years, impeding the country's postwar reconstruction. But anyway, by 1950 many of the Paperclip specialists were given US citizenship or permanent residency. That meant Nazi scientists were able to enter the United States from Latin America.'

'How many are we talking?' asked Joanne.

'In all, around 1,600 scientists and engineers were brought to the US. Plus their families.'

Joanne shook her head in disbelief.

'It gets worse,' said Emma, forcing a smile that conveyed bitterness and cynicism in equal measures. 'Some of the bastards even won awards from NASA and the Defense Department.'

'Like von Braun?' Joanne grimaced.

'The US government would argue that Paperclip was necessary to contain Soviet expansionism. That these scientists achieved important scientific accomplishments.'

'But at what cost?' Joanne challenged.

'Indeed,' nodded Emily. 'The Americans say that Wernher von Braun was chief architect of the Saturn V launch vehicle. Without von Braun there would have been no moon landing. And then there's Adolf Busemann, who designed the swept wing that improved aircraft performance at high speeds.'

There was a long silence. Emily glanced at the shore as the shadows of an early winter dusk fell across the pier.

'It's still disgusting,' said Joanne.

'Yeah,' replied Emily, 'but in 1963 Truman said that he never regretted approving Paperclip. At the time Stalin was imposing communism at gunpoint over eastern Europe.'

'Churchill's Iron Curtain.'

'Precisely,' agreed Emily. 'The Cold War was heating up and the US wanted to prevent the Soviets from accessing those German scientists and their knowledge.'

'So, were any of these Germans ever held to account?' asked Joanne.

'A few were investigated over their Nazi Party membership. But only one scientist was tried and he was acquitted. Another was linked to human experiments at the Ravensbrück concentration camp. But the CIA helped him escape to Argentina.'

Joanne shook her head. 'Unbelievable.'

'Then, in 1984, rocket scientist Arthur Rudolph was accused of using slave labour to build the V-2 missiles at Peenemünde. He cut a deal with the US government to renounce his American citizenship and return to Germany, where he was never prosecuted.'

'So much for the new and democratic Germany,' Joanne sighed.

'The US weren't the only ones to import German scientists and technicians,' said Emily. 'The British got into the act as well. Like the US, they were scared of Stalin and wanted to develop British military strength. Stalin was already breaking his promise to allow democratic elections in eastern Europe. So the British didn't trust the Kremlin's promise not to recruit German rocket scientists. And it was a Labour government in power then.'

'That's right,' nodded Joanne, 'Churchill lost the election of July 1945. Do you think he would have done the same?'

'Probably,' shrugged Emily. 'He certainly didn't trust Stalin and kept trying to convince Roosevelt that the Soviets would be a menace after the war with Germany was won.'

'You're probably right about Churchill.'

'So, in any event, the Brits organised the transfer of leading SS officers and Nazi scientists to Australia.'

'To Australia?' Joanne echoed in a tone of outraged disbelief.

'Yep,' nodded Emily. 'They codenamed it Matchbox. It was the mirror image of the US program. The object was to deny the Soviets access to some of the best German scientists, engineers and soldiers – and never mind their crimes under the Third Reich.'

Joanne's nostrils flared. 'That damned Menzies,' she hissed.

'Actually, it happened mostly under Labor,' said Emily. 'Under Chifley. Menzies only became PM in 1949.'

'But wasn't Chifley a big supporter of Zionism?' challenged Joanne. 'I don't understand.'

'Maybe his support for the establishment of a Jewish state was compensation for secret guilt?' Emily hypothesised. 'But who knows? What we do know is that the program was top secret because the Americans and British didn't want the Soviets to know how many of Germany's best scientific and engineering minds they'd enlisted.'

'I also doubt the Australian public would accept an influx of Nazis in their midst,' mused Joanne. 'At least I hope they wouldn't.'

'True,' nodded Emily. 'I can't imagine this news would have been well received by the RSL just a few years after the war.'

'I guess not,' Joanne agreed. 'All those Rats of Tobruk and veterans of El Alamein would have taken a pretty dim view of resettling Nazis down under.'

'Of course, it all came out many years later,' said Emily. 'In the 1990s, press reports revealed that at least 127 German scientists and engineers were sent to Australia between 1946 and 1951.'

'So, Menzies *was* involved!' said Joanne, with a glint in her eye.

'He inherited the program from Labor,' replied Emily. 'Some of those Germans were given whole new identities. Others worked on missile research and weapon development, despite a blanket ban on

Nazis entering the country. Many were employed at the Woomera rocket range and others at the Salisbury explosives factory, which was a support facility for Woomera.'

'I don't think I'll ever be voting Labor again,' said Joanne.

'I hear you,' said Emily. 'The Simon Wiesenthal Centre says that Australia became a haven for Holocaust perpetrators and demanded an investigation. The Australian Jewish community joined the calls for an official inquiry. They said it was a disgrace that fully paid-up Nazi Party members, including those who belonged to SS killing units, were permitted to enter Australia and start new lives, often at taxpayers' expense.'

'This is all so depressing,' said Joanne in a soft voice. 'But it's good you're teaching this to your students. What was that Santayana quote?'

'"Those who cannot remember the past are condemned to repeat it".' Emily smiled. 'But I'm happy we see the world through the same eyes.'

'Yes, I think we have the same convictions, the same social conscience and commitment to what is right,' replied Joanne, 'if that isn't blowing my own trumpet too much. That's why I feel so comfortable when we're together.'

Emily leant forward and kissed Joanne tenderly.

They smiled and took each other's hand.

Emily lifted her glass, 'To us,' she said quietly with a smile.

They drank.

Shabbat

Friday – the night Jewish people commemorate the Sabbath. On this Shabbat, as on countless other Friday nights, John registered the strange unease he always felt in his mother's house. He had grown up here, and yet it never felt like home. The feeling had grown even stronger after his father's death, when it slowly dawned on John how much his father's warmth and generosity of spirit had enlivened the family.

Sitting at the heavy mahogany table in the dining room, he gazed through the doorway into his mother's study: the shelves of books in alphabetical order, the thick Persian rug, the wheeled stepladder with trinkets or ornaments on each step.

Sarah, his mother, entered the room and bent to kiss him. 'Good Shabbat,' she said.

John inclined his head stiffly. 'Good Shabbat,' he replied, then abruptly stood up. 'Just getting a glass of water,' he said, unable to meet her eye.

Returning from the kitchen, John studied Sarah covertly as she finished setting the table, placing napkins in engraved rings and gleaming silver coasters on the embroidered white linen tablecloth. These last few months he'd noticed a heaviness, almost a lethargy in her movements, but that was hardly surprising: she was eighty-seven. For years her hearing had been so bad she had strained to make out conversations, and now, with her large eyes sunk into dark sockets, she looked quite ill.

John heard the front door open.

'Good Shabbat,' his brother called, his voice echoing down the hall, as he ushered his wife and their two sons, Benjamin and Mark, into the room.

They exchanged the customary greetings, then John turned to Benjamin. 'Mazel-tov,' he said, 'I hear you passed your exams.'

Benjamin grinned, but before he could say anything, John's two children, Rebecca and Joshua, arrived with his wife Deborah. 'Sorry we're late,' she said, 'we waited until the rain eased.'

That Shabbat, like every other, candles stood in silver candlesticks at the head of the table beside the challah and wine. The family was observant, steeped in tradition, treasuring its history, and the customary Jewish way of life. They believed in God, ate kosher food and observed the Sabbath, festivals and holy days. At John's insistence, and despite her protests about being the centre of attention, Sarah agreed to sit at the head of the Shabbat table. For her part, it was an honour she would never have chosen, preferring to remain quietly unnoticed.

John, the younger of Sarah's two sons, sat on her right next to his wife. Maurice, the elder, sat on her left beside his wife, and the four grandchildren, all now young teenagers, were grouped together at the end of the table.

John's daughter Rebecca lit the candles, welcomed the Sabbath and sang the blessing. John lifted the wine glass and said, '*Barukh atah Adonai, Eloheinu, melekh ha-olam, borei p'ri hagafen.*' And translated for the children, 'Praise to You, our God, Sovereign of the universe, Creator of the fruit of the vine.'

John's nephew Mark removed the cover from the challah while reciting the blessing over the bread.

Sarah smiled, glanced at her granddaughter and asked, 'How was school?' Then, before Rebecca could reply, turned to Deborah and said, 'And how was your day?' Not for the first time John considered this woman who talked but said nothing of real significance and seemed unable to listen. Was it just her deafness?

John watched as his mother rested her chin on her palm to hide the faint tremor. She must have been a beauty in her youth, and even in old age she was still striking.

Deborah smiled and said, 'Fine, thanks, and Rebecca handed in that history project, didn't you, honey.'

'I'm doing a history project, too,' Josh offered, 'on my roots. Can I interview you about the war, Nana?'

'No,' Sarah said decisively, and reached for the chopped liver, concentrating a little too hard as she spread it on her challah.

John thought of the many times he had asked his mother the same question, and how she had invariably shut down the conversation or abruptly changed the subject.

Joshua glanced at his mother, puzzled by his grandmother's blunt response.

'Great herring salad, Nana,' Rebecca said, to ease the tension.

'All the other kids in the class are getting help from their grandparents,' Joshua persisted, staring at his grandmother.

'Isn't it time you talked about it, Sarah?' Deborah said gently.

'Yes, Nana, what happened?' said Benjamin.

Sarah muttered to herself, took another bite of challah, then said, 'Enough. I don't want to talk about it.' Her eyes had gone dead, and John realised he had seen this expression on his mother's face before. Her whole face became impassive, blank. She got to her feet wearily. 'Some things should not be talked about,' she said, then left the table and disappeared into the kitchen.

John had no idea of his family history; his whole life had been lived in the shadow of his mother's secrets. His father had talked openly about his own family, mourning the losses, celebrating the few survivals. But his mother had remained mute. Didn't Joshua have a right to know about his heritage? Didn't John himself?

❋

That night John couldn't sleep. He lay beside Deborah and thought about his family's Shabbat meal, his jaw and neck tight as he retraced the conversation.

What was his mother hiding? He thought about her obsession with cleanliness, her insistence that the dusting be done daily, the effort she put into polishing all the silverware till it gleamed.

John recalled a rare beach holiday they'd had when he was a little boy. His mother had scraped a line in the wet sand to mark the boundary of his playground. Of course he'd crossed the line, running gleefully into the towering waves, her hoarse shrieks muffled by the roar of the surf. She'd dragged him roughly from the water, slapped him hard on the backside, her eyes full of panic, her chest heaving from exertion. He'd been frightened of her, but now he realised that her overreaction was an expression of her own dark inner terrors. Remembering her response to Joshua, he realised how rigidly she guarded those terrors.

He eased himself out of bed to fetch a glass of water, resolving to speak to his mother. Joshua had a right to know the family history – they all did. After so many years, he could no longer tolerate his mother's silence. He suddenly felt an urgent need to know her, to try one last time to establish the intimacy that had eluded him throughout his life. After all, they had very little time left.

Next morning John went to see his mother. She opened the door in her loose-fitting pink nightgown, her face stripped of make-up. She looked weary, vulnerable and small. Although she was surprised to see him, she didn't comment on his unannounced visit.

'Can I come in?' John asked after a short silence.

'Of course.' She stepped back and ushered him into the house.

Taking a seat at the kitchen table, John said, 'We need to talk.'

'If it is about last night, there is nothing to say,' Sarah said. 'You want coffee?'

'Thank you. And yes, there is. You upset Joshua.'

'I know, I know,' Sarah sighed. 'I'm sorry. I don't know…'

Looking at his frail old mother, John was momentarily lost for words. How to begin to ask the questions that had for so long gone unasked?

'Tell me about your parents,' he said suddenly, before he had time to think.

Sarah's eyes narrowed. 'Why? What purpose does it serve?' She was quiet a long time, staring blankly out of the window.

John watched her, patiently waiting for her to speak.

Eventually she sighed heavily. 'All right,' she said brusquely. 'My father was a merchant – a successful businessman, self-made. He imported silk from Italy and France into Poland. He was a cultured man. He had seats at the theatre and the opera and he would host politicians and visitors from abroad. Yitzhak Gruenbaum, the leader of the Zionist faction in the Polish Parliament, loved going to the opera, and often accompanied my parents. Our family had influence. We had respectability…status. In Warsaw, before Hitler, we were the social elite.'

John leaned in as Sarah spoke, encouraged, even astonished, that she had finally shared some small part of her past.

'Did you live in a big house?' he asked.

Sarah regarded John silently for several moments. 'What do you want from me?' she said.

John held her gaze, waiting for her to continue.

'We had an apartment, on the third floor,' she said, leaning her forearms on the table. 'It overlooked a boulevard lined with big trees. It was not like the Jewish area – the plantation in the centre had shrubs and flowers. When I sat at the piano in the living room I could look out over the park. The rooms were big, with high ceilings, and we had paintings – some beautiful paintings. My mother had a maidservant to polish her silver and clean the crystal. My father sent us to a Jewish school and employed private tutors to come to our home to teach us drawing or music. He employed a French governess to teach us French and needlework and take us to school. My sister was two years older than me. Each Friday a man would do errands for our family.' She paused thoughtfully. 'We had a good life…and we were happy. My parents were kind…' Her voice faded and she stared unseeing at her hands, twisting and crumpling some invisible cloth.

John hesitated, then took a deep breath and said, 'Tell me what happened.'

Sarah reached for her coffee cup, her hand trembling. When she finally spoke, her voice was husky and low. 'One day my father asked me to run an errand. I was fifteen.' She took a sip of coffee.

'The Nazis snatched me off the street,' she said. 'I was taken to Nazi headquarters. They had the lot there – crystal chandeliers, wood panelling, paintings, mirrors…I remember there were waiters carrying trays of wine and beer, and the men were singing.' Sarah seemed lost in thought. 'I remember the uniforms, the red armbands, the black leather boots…swastikas…'

John leant across and took her hand, stroking the thin papery skin. It was the first time he had touched her hand in years.

'They escorted me from the room…they took turns,' she said, tears running down the lines in her cheeks.

John tried to imagine the terror of a fifteen-year-old girl, momentarily pictured his own daughter, but shied away from the image in revulsion.

'I lost count of the number of nights,' Sarah said, her voice cracking.

John felt a dark horror move through him.

'One morning I went to the bathroom, grabbed a razor blade, and cut off great chunks of my hair until I was almost bald. That afternoon three of them raped me. That was my punishment,' she continued.

John looked at his mother, his eyes filled with tears. 'I'm so sorry,' he said hoarsely. It was all he could think of to say.

'After the war I learned about the gas chambers of Treblinka, Auschwitz, and the mass slaughter of Jews in the Ponary Forest,' Sarah continued.

John tried to think about the murdered millions, but it was too vast, too appalling. His own mother's suffering was less easy to evade.

The Nazis might have tried to destroy Sarah's spirit, but her children and grandchildren were testament to her defiance of the Nazis' genocidal aspirations. Some words from *My Name is Asher Lev* came to him then: 'To kill a human being is to kill also the children and children's children that might have come from him down through all the generations.'

'I never spoke about what happened to me,' Sarah explained. 'I couldn't. It was the only way I could live. More than anything, I think about my parents and what they must have felt that night when I didn't return. I never saw them again. They all died without knowing I had survived.'

John was overwhelmed with compassion for his mother. Finally he asked her, 'And Dad, did he know?'

Sarah placed her trembling hands in her lap. 'I told him. I had to,' she said. 'It…affected us.'

John swallowed hard, his head starting to pound, and a heaviness gathered in his chest. 'I'll just be a moment,' he said, walking down the hallway to the bathroom. He splashed water on his face, collected himself and returned to the kitchen.

'You try to convince yourself that you are a victim, that it's not your fault,' Sarah continued, 'but deep down you feel guilty – soiled. It weighed on me, ate at me like a cancer.'

'Guilty? What do you mean guilty?' John asked.

'Guilty that I couldn't give your father what he needed,' Sarah said, her head bowed.

John put his arm around his mother and felt her frail shoulders lose a little of their tension. She seemed emotionally depleted, but perhaps this unburdening after so many years would eventually bring her some relief.

'You've carried this for so long – almost your entire life. You needed to talk, Mum,' he said gently.

Lifting her head, Sarah smiled wanly at her son. She reached for the challah from the previous night and tore off a piece. 'I love seeing you all,' she said, before taking a bite, 'my family, my grandchildren, with their smiles, their laughter…I love Shabbat.'

The Girl on the Passport

I arrived at 26A Ogrodowa Ulica in Warsaw at two in the afternoon. It was a four-storey art deco building with the ubiquitous grey concrete render and white-framed windows of the Communist era. The street was lined with similar buildings, and leafy trees cast shadows onto parked cars and a stretch of lawn bordering the footpath. Children played on the grass and a dog barked.

I walked through a wide archway that led to a paved courtyard and turned into a narrow corridor. The apartment was at the end of the hall, and I could smell chicken soup wafting through a half-open window.

I knocked and heard a door open and close and footsteps – someone was home at least, and coming to the door.

I felt a sudden sense of unreality. It was as if all the previous years of my life had led me somehow to this moment, and all the future years of my life would depend on its outcome. I stood there for a moment, heart thudding, feeling suddenly uncertain. Then I took a deep breath and the feeling passed.

A tall, sophisticated woman opened the door, head erect, short grey hair brushed back from her face – this must be Hannah. She looked to be in her mid-seventies, with a sculpted face and a warm smile. It was a gentle face and I liked her immediately. Her eyes were wide and pale blue, not what I'd expected for a Jewish woman. She was wearing a black pleated skirt, white blouse, camel cardigan and tan silk scarf.

She looked at me and her eyes seemed to search my face for a long time. Then she smiled faintly and said in Polish, 'Yes, can I help you?'

Hesitating, I asked, 'Are you Hannah?'

She nodded cautiously. 'Who are you?'

'My name is Ronald, I'm your cousin – your father's nephew.'

She looked a little uncertain. I didn't want to make her any more uncomfortable so I said, 'My father told me lots of stories about the Warsaw Ghetto – about you and him.'

She breathed in sharply, and her face paled.

'Can we talk?'

She stared at me for a moment, then covered her mouth with a handkerchief and coughed, a deep, rasping cough that shook her slender body. When the coughing stopped she took off her glasses and wiped her eyes, then she put her glasses back on, and smiled at me.

'Come in,' she said, tears washing down her cheeks.

She wrapped her arm around mine and walked me down a strip of carpet that ran the length of the hall. We passed a bathroom, a telephone stand, a wall of family photos and then we were in the lounge room, where one wall was lined with floor-to-ceiling bookcases. Along the opposite wall were curtained windows that looked onto the main street, and in the corner of the room stood a grand piano. Magazines were piled on the coffee table in the centre of the room.

Hannah looked at me and smiled. 'Are you hungry?'

'No, I've just eaten.'

'Can I offer you tea?'

'Yes please.'

'Take a seat.'

I watched as she left the room, returning a few minutes later with a tray of tea things and biscuits. While she was busy with the teapot I said, 'Tell me about my father.'

She was holding a cup of tea in one hand, the bottom of the cup resting on her other palm. She hesitated, then put the cup on the low table, looked at me and was silent for so long I thought she might not speak at all. She filled her own cup and, putting a cube of sugar between her teeth, she sipped slowly, letting the tea soak through the sugar. I could see she was collecting her thoughts, perhaps wondering where to begin. 'What can I say?' Her soft voice broke, and the last word came out husky.

'Tell me about the Warsaw Ghetto.'

Hannah sat for a long time, looking first at me, then out the window, then back to me. I could see she was nervous.

'How did you and Dad get separated?'

She lifted her head to look at me and I saw her eyes were sad.

Later, when she finished speaking, she seemed to withdraw into herself. I didn't know what to say. I forced a smile. Hannah seemed tired and her eyes were misty. She picked up her cup, then put it down again. Finally she looked at her watch and said, 'It's getting late.'

'Can we continue tomorrow?'

'Of course,' she said. 'Thank you for coming to see me.' Her voice trembled.

Three months earlier I could never have imagined I would be sitting in a Warsaw apartment with a cousin I had never known, or that she would have such a story to tell.

'So, what's planned for LA?' I said. It was winter, 2000, and we'd all recovered from our fear of flying when no planes fell from the sky on New Year's Day, despite apocalyptic warnings in the lead-up to the new millennium.

Judy put her finger to her lips, indicating the kids, who were slumped in their seats.

'Disneyland, Universal Studios, the Getty Centre and the Museum of Tolerance.'

I looked at her. 'You're joking. The Museum of Tolerance?'

'It's one of the best Holocaust museums in the world.'

'It's the last place I want to spend my holidays,' I said.

'Everybody says it's a must.'

I considered this for a moment. 'But this is meant to be fun,' I said, hearing the plaintive note in my voice.

Judy just looked at me.

I forced myself to meet her gaze. 'And the kids, will they be interested?'

'They need to understand their heritage, what it means to be Jewish,' Judy said.

'That's why you insisted we send them to a Jewish school,' I said.

'*You* chose Mount Scopus, not me, remember. It does a good job with the Holocaust.'

'Fine,' she said. 'Don't come.'

Silence. It seemed the subject was closed. This was the point at which I usually gave in, but instead I turned to the window and shut my eyes. The voices of the kids in the seats behind grated and the thought of having to spend a day at the Museum of Tolerance irritated me. Clearly I wasn't going to be able to sleep, at least not for a while. And it wasn't that I didn't want to know about the Holocaust, it was that I already knew too much.

As kids, my sister and I had spent many bedtime hours with Mum talking about the Holocaust. Most children listened to *Snugglepot and Cuddlepie* at bedtime, but not us. I lost count of the number of times Mum said, 'You were named after your father's brother – he was a gifted pianist. We lost him at Treblinka, with so many others.'

I remembered my parents' response when, at eighteen, I told them I didn't want to go to university, I wanted to become a musician. Mum was standing at the sink with her back to me and Dad was sitting at the table in his pyjamas. 'You're not leaving school,' he said. 'Fine, go to the conservatorium and study real music, but you're not going to throw away your life.'

I stared at my toast.

'When we came to Australia we had nothing. The Nazis deprived me of an education but I worked hard and made something of myself just so we could be financially secure. Education is important. Lawyers, doctors, earn good money. How much money do you think you'll get playing the guitar?' he demanded.

I remember leaving the kitchen, wanting to run away from the house and its oppressive atmosphere of guilt and ghosts. It seemed that every aspect of my past, and now my future, was contaminated by the Holocaust.

※

It was drizzling lightly when we arrived at the Museum of Tolerance. In the end I had decided to come out of respect for those who had died and those who had survived the camps. I also wanted to avoid having to justify my absence to my children, which might have opened up the subject of my childhood and my family. You could say I took the path of least resistance.

The brown building was unobtrusive. Five leafy trees in planter boxes stood in front of what looked like stepped shipping containers. Inside it was stark, sterile and cold and the visitors' faces were solemn.

After we'd left our coats and bags, I turned to Judy and said, 'These old guides remind me of my father.'

'I understand this is hard for you, Ron, but think of the children,' Judy said.

'There is plenty of time for them to learn about such horrors; does it have to be now?'

Judy ignored me.

We were ushered downstairs to an open auditorium where we were subjected to an orientation. Our guide rattled out a stream of statistics and droned on about the themes of the museum; he described the Holocaust as 'the ultimate example of man's inhumanity to man'.

The briefing over, we were set free. Walking past the section on the Cambodian atrocities and Armenian genocide, we arrived at the Holocaust section. As we entered, each of us received a photo passport; mine belonged to a young girl, who looked to be about thirteen years old, with dark eyes and olive skin. According to the brief description on the card, she was born in Warsaw, like my father.

'Another horrible Holocaust story. I can't stand it,' I muttered and put the passport in my pocket.

Next, we were herded together and a timed tour moved us to an exhibit titled, 'The Rise and Fall of the Third Reich'. We stood in front of a re-creation of a 1930s Berlin café where people were discussing Hitler's rise to power and the Nazi takeover of Germany. I imagined the couple at the table were my paternal grandparents. As if reading my mind, my son Adam said to me, 'Were your parents from Germany or Poland, Dad?'

'Warsaw, but my mother escaped to Russia – that's how she survived.'

'And your father?' my daughter asked.

'He wasn't so lucky, Romy.'

'Did you know your grandparents?' Adam asked.

'No,' I said. 'And I'm glad I didn't.'

'Why?' he asked, gazing up at me, his face registering his disapproval.

'My father was so enmeshed in the past – never able to move beyond the Holocaust – I think he got most of his *meshugas* from his parents, although he endured a lot.'

'But it wasn't their fault,' Adam said.

'I know it wasn't deliberate, but growing up with that was hard,' I said. 'My dad had enough problems of his own without having to carry his parents' problems as well.'

'Can you tell us a bit about them?' Romy asked.

'Well, briefly, my paternal grandfather was a merchant. They were a well-to-do family who lived in the part of Warsaw that later became the Jewish ghetto.'

'Why didn't they leave before the war?' Romy asked.

I sighed. 'I don't know. Maybe they thought their connections would protect them or maybe they didn't realise how bad it would get. Who could have known what lay ahead...?'

Romy leaned forward and nodded, encouraging me to continue.

'But had they left, my life would have been very different – much happier – and so would their life, *and* my father's. But who knew?'

Romy looked at me and frowned. Turning away, I said to Judy, 'I need a coffee – I'll see you at the next exhibit.'

'Are you all right?'

'I'll be fine,' I snapped.

'Maybe a double scotch?'

I forced a smile and turned towards the café.

As I sat drinking my coffee, I remembered one Shabbat when I was about fifteen. At the table that evening Dad had been subdued. He kept staring at me throughout the meal, looking as if he was on the verge of tears. At one point, after a long silence, he said, 'If there was a God he would have saved those six million Jews.'

Before I went to sleep that night I asked my mother, 'What was the matter with Dad at dinner?'

'Today is the anniversary of his brother's disappearance.'

'Oh, that's really sad,' I said.

'Yes,' she replied.

A waiter came and collected my empty coffee cup, pulling me back to the present. I realised I needed to return to my family.

I found them in the information room where visitors were inserting their passports into a computer to receive an update on their person's life. Judy turned and looked at me. 'Better now?' she said.

I shrugged.

The kids queued to put their passports into the computer, but I held back, not wanting to know what had happened to the girl whose life story was in my pocket.

'Did you get your printout, Dad?' Romy asked.

Once again, I decided that it was easier to go along with them than to protest and draw attention to myself. With a sigh, I inserted my photo passport into the computer and received a printout of the child's experiences.

I learned she had been forced into the Warsaw Ghetto with her grandmother along with 400,000 other Jews. The printout explained that the girl had come from an affluent family, but in the ghetto she shared a room with ten others, was often hungry and could not sleep at night.

Reading her story reminded me of Hannah, my father's niece. I had heard her story many times during my childhood. Hannah's parents had left Warsaw for Vilna on a business trip, just before the German offensive, and then couldn't return. She was left in the safekeeping of my father. The two of them escaped the deportations and ended up in the Warsaw Ghetto, where my father found work as a tailor. During the day Hannah was free to clamber through the tunnels that connected the ghetto with the 'Aryan' side to scavenge for food.

One day, when my father returned from work, Hannah was not waiting for him. A few people said they had seen her disappear through the gates of the ghetto. My father told me he made many attempts to get to the Polish side to find her, but it was impossible. He eventually gave up hope for his niece, convinced she had been shot by the Nazis. Soon after, my father was relocated to Majdanek, a death camp, where he was used as slave labour. He eventually ended up in Auschwitz.

Judy and the kids had followed the guide to an interactive exhibit and were listening to a survivor's recorded testimony. I tuned out and thought again of my father. When I buried him fifteen years ago, I had made a conscious decision to close the door on the oppressiveness of my family's past and my own childhood. But now, in this museum, it was all rushing back. I felt that familiar heaviness in my chest, as if I were being suffocated.

I started walking towards the café to escape from it all, but I could not forget the face of my young girl and my pace slowed. It felt disrespectful not to honour her experience, not to understand her story. I took out her passport and continued reading about her life.

Like Dad and Hannah, she had fought in the Warsaw Ghetto Uprising of April 1943. Surprised, I looked again at her photograph: she did not seem old enough. But I remembered my father telling me that most of the Jewish soldiers of the uprising had been little more than children, and their commander, Mordechai Anielewicz, was in his early twenties when the insurrection took place. I had always imagined my father's niece as daring, brave and full of hope – just like the girl on the passport. Having made the connection between her and Hannah, I felt compelled to continue through the exhibits.

As I followed her story, I learned that she had not survived the war. Everyone assumed that she had perished during the fighting in the ghetto uprising; whatever the case, she was never seen again.

We followed our guide to the Hall of Testimony where we witnessed the stories of many survivors. It was an empty, cold room and the sprinklers on the ceiling reminded me of the gas chambers. I shuddered at the thought of my family, my people, moments before their death – all my father's uncles, aunts and their children – who were sent to Treblinka. I had thought that hearing countless stories about the Holocaust as a kid had inured me to its horrors.

From the Hall of Testimony we moved on to our next stop: a re-creation of the death camp of Auschwitz. The exhibit was deliberately dirty, dark and surrounded with barbed wire. An eerie silence had fallen on the people looking at it.

As we entered the exhibit we were confronted with two lanes – one for the small number of people deemed able to work and the other for the majority of victims: women, children and the elderly who were sent to the gas chambers on arrival. In many cases, the entire transport was sent to their immediate death.

I pictured my father there, for this is where he had ended up. He saw crowds of people driven and whipped through the camp to the gas chambers.

A plaque on the wall described the work of the *Sondercommandos*: a group of Jewish men who were forced to calm the people on arrival, selecting those for the gas chambers, sorting the victims' possessions and later removing corpses. Very few of these men survived because they were witnesses to the genocide, but those who did survive lived with the guilt of having sent fellow Jews to their deaths. And many survivors accused them of being complicit with the Nazis.

As I stood there looking at the exhibit, I started to appreciate, really for the first time, the extent of my father's torment. He had been a member of the *Sonderkommando*. He had survived but was plagued with survivor guilt.

A memory suddenly came to me: I was in Acland Street with Dad on a Sunday morning when a group of men spat at us as we walked past. 'Shame on you,' they hissed. My father refused to talk about the incident, and would not explain why it had happened.

I looked across at Adam who was clearly struggling to comprehend the incomprehensible. I thought of my dead father who had tried to make me understand. He had suffered and I had suffered because of his suffering. He was unable to show love or compassion or empathy. After he had lost everyone and found himself alone, he seemed afraid to allow himself to love again. I wondered whether Hannah's survival would have made things different for him.

We left the Holocaust exhibition, but Judy and the children were keen to see other parts of the museum. It was too much for me: I needed time to compose myself, to free myself from the unsought recollections of my father and the memories of my childhood.

I noticed feedback cards near the door so I sat down to complete one. In the space provided for additional comments, I felt compelled to write something of my father's story. I also described how the young girl's passport had affected me, how she had reminded me of my cousin, Hannah.

Cousin: I realised that I had used the word for the first time. Yes, she was my cousin.

We left the museum and continued our holiday, but my father's ghost haunted me and I could not stop thinking about him. I regretted allowing the years to drift by; I regretted how seldom we had spoken, how little we'd shared of ourselves; I regretted not taking the time to pick up the phone or visit.

Three months after our return, I received a letter from the director of the museum. Initially I mistook it for an advertising brochure and was about to toss it in the bin when I saw 'Private and Confidential' marked in red on the envelope.

One of the museum researchers had read my family story and believed she had some information about a close relative. The woman was now in her seventies and had been raised in Poland as a Christian after the war. She had made contact with Jewish organisations in Israel and America in the hope of discovering information about her family, who had died during the Holocaust. The researcher believed that this woman was my cousin.

I was stunned. My mind raced with a million questions as I picked up the phone to call the museum. I could not turn my back on this. Here was the link to my father's world; I was sure this was Hannah. I needed to know more, to make contact, to hear about her, and to see her. She would tell me what had happened. I would discover it on my father's behalf.

Two days later I was on a plane to Poland.

'Good morning,' I said as Hannah opened the door.

She looked thin and worn, her eyes red in her pale face. She looked as if she hadn't slept all night. 'Come in,' she said in a low voice, smiling faintly.

I followed her down the hall, resumed my seat from the previous day and watched her pour tea. After passing a cup to me she filled her own cup and took a sugar cube. Then she put the cup down and nodded as if to say, let's start.

'Thank you for taking the time to see me,' I said.

'You're family, how could I not?'

'How did you and Dad get separated?' I hadn't meant to blurt out such a question. There was a long moment of silence. When she finally spoke, her voice was warm.

'I'll never forget that day. It was the eve of Passover – 19 April 1943. I remember it was around four in the afternoon when I tried to get back into the ghetto. But the uprising had started and it was impossible to get past the SS. I was forced to stay on the Aryan side, so I went to see friends of my parents for help and luckily they were willing to look after me. I spent the rest of the war hiding in their cellar.'

Hannah lifted her head and looked at me for a long moment. She seemed to be searching for something she had been missing for a long time.

'My life under the occupation and after the war was very hard. From the moment I lost my parents my path was strewn with tears.'

She looked down at the floor as she spoke and her voice was seared with pain.

'I was left alone after the war, not equipped for life, helpless, without any means. I worked in various offices – I knew Russian and French well...'

She spoke quietly now, as if all this were routine.

'Shortly after the war, there were more pogroms and Jews started leaving Poland – all heading towards Israel. I was so alone I was frightened – I was in a terrible situation.'

I sat waiting as her sad eyes fixed on mine.

'I could not remain in Poland but I had no way out. It was a time when single women were getting married just to escape this second hell. After long deliberations and against my better judgement, I also decided to take this step, in order to survive.'

I felt my throat constricting. Even after the war this woman had suffered. She finished her tea and said, almost as if she was talking to herself, 'Sometimes I get the feeling we're nothing more than ants to be trodden on.' She no longer seemed to see me.

'I left for Israel – foreign country, strange people, heavy climate – and there I fell into another misery. The man I married turned out to be evil and despotic, he treated me badly. Once more I walked on a tear-strewn path. In those days I was remembering my lost family, whose memory will always stay with me, and those people dear to them, and therefore dear to me.'

I could not hold back the tears. When Hannah spoke next her voice was low and subdued. 'At the moment when there seems to be no meaning in life, one needs to find a new meaning. For a few years I was completely depressed, physically and mentally. The doctors advised me to go back to Poland, so I started to think how to escape, how to leave Israel.'

She gazed out the window and I had the feeling she wasn't so much talking to me as to herself.

'And so, I arrived back in Warsaw, the city where I spent those happy years with my family. I found my old friends from before the war, met a wonderful, kind man and we had two much-loved children.'

I sat very still on the chair and thought about her words and my late father. What would it have meant to him to know that Hannah had lived?

'My husband passed away a few years ago and my son, a merchant banker, lives with his wife and children in New York. My daughter, a professor of literature at Oxford, lives with her family outside London.'

I could hear the soft rustling of the curtains as they shifted in the breeze from the open window.

My mood had shifted too. Now I felt a complex mix of happiness for Hannah that her life had been worth living, and sorrow for all that she had lost – that we had lost. I began to weep, but this time the tears were not just for the suffering she had endured.

'So, that is the story of my life, in brief.' She turned her head and looked out the window and we sat in silence for a moment. It was an easy silence, not awkward. Then she said, 'And now, I want to know about your father: how he survived the uprising, how he escaped from the ghetto, when he left Poland, how he settled in Australia, his family and so much more. He was such a dear man – so funny.'

Picture Credits

- Dealing with the Devil: Packing oranges in Petach Tikva; PikiWiki Israel 2521, Wikipedia; courtesy משפחת סלור.

- Night of Broken Glass: Civilians watch a Kristallnacht Nazi officer vandalise Jewish property, most likely in Fürth, outside Nuremberg; Wikipedia

- Finding Home: Refugees on the ship *St Louis*, South Hampton, England; Archives, Yad Vashem: the World Holocaust Remembrance Center; https://collections.yadvashem.org/en/photos/84209

- The Good Brother: Albert Göring, Wikipedia

- Never Forget: Emanual Ringelblum: Wikipedia

- Wannsee Conference – Protocol: Reichsführer SS Heinrich Himmler and his colleagues at a meeting; from left: Franz Josef Huber (secret state police), Arthur Nebe (criminal investigation department), Heinrich Himmler, Reinhard Heydrich (security service); and Heinrich Müller (secret state police, also known as Gestapo-Müller); photo by ullstein bild via Getty Images

- To Kill the Führer: Field Marshal Erwin Rommel, c. 1942: Wikipedia, courtesy German Federal Archive (Deutsches Bundesarchiv)

- The Warsaw Ghetto Uprising: Photo by Hulton Archive/Getty Images

- The Secret Stain: Project Paperclip Team at Fort Bliss, including Wernher von Braun (front row, seventh from right); Wikipedia

- Shabbat: Gola Mire, a member of the Polish Workers Party, Zionist Youth Organisation and Jewish Resistance; unlike her contemporary, Sarah, she did not survive the war; Wikipedia, https://creativecommons.org/licenses/by-sa/3.0/

- The Girl on the Passport: passport card assembled using a photograph of Helena Weissblatt, courtesy the Museum of Tolerance

Every effort has been made to discover and contact copyright holders of images reproduced in this book. We would be pleased to correct any omissions should they be drawn to our attention.

About the Author

BERNARD MARIN AM was born in 1950 and graduated from the Prahran College of Advanced Education in Melbourne in 1970. He established his accounting practice in 1981 and currently works with the staff and partners of the practice as a consultant. Bernard lives in Melbourne with his wife, Wendy.

Other books by Bernard:

My Father, My Father

Good as Gold

Stories of Profit and Loss

Stories of Remembering and Forgetting

Letter to my Father

People Who Have Changed the World: Imagined interviews

We Had A Dream

Breakfast with Paul: We Beg To Differ; Surviving: My Story

These titles can be found at:

bernardmarin.com.au

Acknowledgments

In writing these interviews I was fortunate to have the support of many people.

I am grateful for the help of my editors. Nan McNab's extensive work in editing these interviews has been instrumental in making them infinitely better. I have greatly benefited from her insights, counsel and assistance. She has been remarkably patient with me, nothing was too difficult, and she was a pleasure to work with. I owe a huge debt of gratitude to Sharon Lapkin for her incredibly generous support. I am truly grateful to her. She gave willingly of her time and I have benefited from her understanding, acumen and direction. She also has made this book immeasurably better.

Finally, many friends have been there for me along this journey. They are too numerous to name – you know who you are. Thank you for your support and encouragement. And last but not least, thank you to my family who have helped me keep everything in perspective.